T0149901

Murder
at the
Movies

A.E. Eddenden

**Academy Chicago
Publishers**

Academy Chicago Publishers
363 West Erie Street
Chicago, Illinois 60610

Printed and bound in the U.S.A.

Library of Congress Cataloging-in-Publication Data

Eddenden, A. E.
    Murder at the movies / A.E. Eddenden
       p.   cm.
    ISBN 0-89733-428-0
    I. Title.
PR9199.3.E32M79   1996
813'.54—dc20   95-50689
                                              CIP

To Michael Frederick

Chapter

1

Inspector Albert V. Tretheway loved the movies. So did Jake. Although Tretheway was an astute critic of most films, Jake was the true trivia buff and plodding historian. He'd never seen a movie he didn't like. And he could recite verbatim passages from his favourites and not so favourites.

The two of them saw more than their share of movies at the West End, a neighbourhood theatre in, naturally, the west end of Fort York. Every Monday and Thursday the double feature bill with added attractions changed. The addeds were world news, previews, possibly a cartoon and a short subject like *The March of Time, Bobby Jones On Golf, Archery With Howard Hill* or a Pete Smith specialty. At the Saturday matinee the features were replaced with more suitable adventure films and the news with an edge-of-the-seat serial, usually one of the fifteen episodes.

This totalled over two hundred feature films a year, not counting Saturdays. Taking into account vacations, sickness, personal preferences (Tretheway disliked Shirley Temple), some seasonal holidays and, in rare instances, business, Tretheway and Jake averaged one hundred movies a year. And 1939 was a bumper year.

●　●　●

"What's on tonight?" Tretheway asked. He sat in the warmth of Addie's kitchen. The standard size chair seemed inadequate for his full 6'5" frame and ample 290 pounds. Spread out before him on the round, dark oak table was the first section of the Monday Fort York *Expositor*. Jake was leaning against the ice box reading the movie pages.

"Looks real good," Jake said. "*The Hound Of The Baskervilles*. Basil Rathbone, Nigel Bruce from the novel by Conan Doyle."

"Sherlock Holmes, my favourite detective," Tretheway said. "Except for Wan Ho."

The two smiled.

"What's the other feature?" Tretheway asked.

"A Laurel and Hardy."

"Never made a bad picture in their lives."

"*Flying Deuces*," Jake read. He checked the wall clock. "It starts in thirty minutes."

"Perfect." Tretheway stood up and stretched. His grey sweatshirt, emblazoned Cleveland Police Games 1937, hiked above his uniform trousers to reveal the striped material of a regulation police-issue collarless shirt. "Just time for a brew, Jake?"

Chapter One

"No thanks. I'm still full." Jake rubbed his flat stomach. At 5'8" 145 pounds, he filled up a lot quicker than his boss. "Great dinner, Addie."

Adelaide Tretheway smiled. Her back was toward the two men as she stood at the sink washing the dishes. She liked to cook and was good at it; simple, English, stick-to-your-ribs fare. Which was probably why she carried a few extra pounds on her sturdy but shapely figure. She was four years younger than her brother Albert, who would turn thirty-nine this year (easy to remember their mother used to say, as old as the century), but admitted only to four less than that, which made her unofficially the same age as Jake.

Addie turned from her task. She pushed curly wisps of brown hair touched with ginger away from her forehead with the back of her soapy hand. When she smiled, as she did now, impishly, lips pressed together barely turning up at the edges, it accentuated the permanent laugh lines around her luminous green eyes. Jake saw nothing else in the room.

"You two," Addie clucked. "When it comes to the movies, you're like a couple of kids."

"I take it you're not joining us?" Tretheway said.

Addie shook her head. "No, thank you."

She seldom went with them but they always invited her. They knew she wouldn't be left alone, what with the half dozen student boarders. Some could be heard now setting the banquet-sized dining room table for tomorrow's breakfast. Addie ran a comfortably disciplined home-away-from-home for students, mostly from nearby Fort York University. The small but reputable school unleashed about four hundred Arts and Theology graduates on the population of Southern

Ontario each year. Its distinguished alumni boasted several cabinet ministers, church and industry leaders, a few professional football players and, Addie's favourite, Constable Jonathan Small. Jake had joined Fort York's finest immediately upon graduation, earning the indisputable long time boarder award.

"It'd be a different story if Nelson Eddy was in the movie." Jake winked at Tretheway.

"Or Charles Boyer," Tretheway said.

Addie ignored their remarks. "Better wrap up," she said. "It's below freezing."

Tretheway looked out the back window. "But no wind to speak of."

"Shall I warm up the car?" Jake asked.

"I think not." Tretheway stood up and drained his Molson's Blue. "Great night for shank's mare." He pushed out through the swinging door on his way to the hall closet.

"For polar bears maybe," Jake grumbled to Addie.

"The walk'll do you good," she said.

● ● ●

Bright moonlight threw Mutt and Jeff shadows of Tretheway and Jake across the unshovelled sidewalks as their stout police boots crunched coldly on the snow. They both wore long, heavy greatcoats. Jake's woolen muffler, wrapped several times around his neck, matched his mitts, hand knit by Addie. A toque pulled low over his ears made up the set. Tretheway's bowler, set dead level on his head, and his white silk scarf were more fashionable than protective. Black leather senior officer's gloves warmed his hands. The West End Theatre was a frosty, good half mile from the Tretheway house.

"Invigorating." Tretheway's breath hung frozen in the January air.

Cold, Jake thought. Every three or four steps he had to take an extra hop skip to keep up with his boss's giant strides.

The two stopped dutifully at each residential intersection and looked both ways before crossing the street. "In case any children are watching," Tretheway would say. Not long ago, as Inspector of the Traffic Division, FYPD, he'd founded a safety club for public school children. "Set an example," he'd explain.

● ● ●

They turned automatically into the candy store on King Street not far from the show. Tretheway bought his usual bag of multi-coloured, hard gum drops, which he always paid for even though Jake shared about ten percent of them. At the box office, Tretheway clicked down his quarter on the cold, black marble counter.

"How do the flicks look tonight, Vi?"

"You'll love 'em," Violet said. "Specially the Sherlock Holmes."

Violet Farrago had been the ticket lady as long as Tretheway could remember. And he remembered her as always middle-aged. She was a tall girl, wide through the torso, birdy legs, naturally frizzy blonde hair, a ready smile and a loud generous laugh. Her normal speaking voice had risen in decibels over the years as her hearing worsened. Violet's glittering, warm grey eyes bulged intently at moving lips during conversations. She had little patience for men with bushy moustaches or beards or for anyone who mumbled.

"Where's your friend?" she asked Tretheway.

"Hi, Vi." Jake emerged from behind his boss and pushed his twenty-five cents forward. "That's a cold one tonight."

"Pardon?"

In addition to having a moustache, Jake tended to mumble. He raised his voice. "I said it's cold out."

"It ain't summer."

Tretheway and Jake pushed through the foyer doors. Their footsteps resounded on the terrazo floor as they walked up the slight incline under the theatre's high, vaulted, intricately ribbed ceiling muralled with scenes of naked cherubs gambolling against a background of fleecy clouds and unnaturally blue skies. On both walls plaster oblongs framed posters of coming attractions. The projectionist crossed their path on his way upstairs. Neil Heavenly stopped biting his nails long enough to nod cordially. Tretheway and Jake waved back.

At the inner lobby doors, Freeman Thake tore their tickets in half with his usual flourish and greeted them officially.

"Good evening, gentlemen."

"Freeman," Tretheway responded. Jake nodded.

Freeman Thake owned and supervised, on a random rotation basis, three neighbourhood movie houses in the Fort York area. The West End was his favourite. He lived with his family in a substantial older home on Melrose Avenue, an affluent street in the city's east end. His success in business was due to his knowledge of people. He knew instinctively when to chide, praise, cajole, argue, sympathize and sometimes even discipline his charges. Thake's dark, sparkling eyes showed an interest in questions most folks considered rhetorical. He charmed his female patrons, puffed up the men and opened doors gracefully for both with no sense of toadying. Overall, he exuded an aura of well-tailored, shoe-shined cleanliness. His jaw was strong, his face deeply tanned, but his very thick, curly black hair, peppered with grey, made his head appear too large for his short smallish frame.

"We're just in time," Jake said.

"Four minutes to curtain," Thake announced.

"Enjoy your adventure." He held the doors open. Tretheway and Jake stepped into semi-darkness.

Lulu Ashcroft took over where Thake left off. They followed her and the meandering bright circle from her flashlight over the thick, silent carpeting of the inner lobby. Jake couldn't help but notice the way the cloth of her suit strained across her quivering rear. She was a big girl with a large chest and, unfortunately, a large everything else, including her waist. Three times a week she enjoyed home-baked beans with heavy brown bread accompanied in the inclement weather by hot rum. She spoke in a soft, lilting, occupational whisper.

They marched past the first aisle where Lulu's fellow usher, Joshua Pike, saluted them with his flashlight and the customary mock bow from the waist that he always gave his favourite regulars. His perpetual blinding smile showed plainly in the dim light. Pike winked at Lulu. She led her two patrons around the corner of the second aisle and stopped almost immediately.

"I saved your seats," Lulu whispered. Her light illuminated the first seat in the back row.

"Thanks Lulu," Tretheway said. He let Jake go in first, then wriggled comfortably into the jumbo seat.

A few years ago, Thake had replaced some of the worn or vandalized aisle seats with what a convincing theatre furniture salesman had called "love seats." They hadn't worked out. The patrons of the West End frowned on their suggested function and those who would have liked to use them were too embarrassed to do it. But one love seat was perfect for one big man.

There was a dark stain on the stuccoed wall behind the seat where Tretheway's brilliantined head had rested during numerous past performances. Tretheway jammed his bowler, upside down, between the two seats, and emptied the large bag of candy into the hat. They seldom ate them all. At any time of year in the Tretheway house, colourful, misshapen balls of stuck-together gum drops could be seen in Addie's candy dishes. The two men settled down, their overcoats and accessories piled warmly on their laps.

The lights dimmed. Foot shuffling and squirming stopped. Conversations ceased expectantly. Suddenly the screen came to life. The large HR trademark faded into the title, *The Flying Deuces.* "Dance Of The Cuckoos" bounced from the speakers. Stan and Ollie sat in a sophisticated, Paris sidewalk cafe exchanging confidences over a glass of milk with two straws . . .

Tretheway and Jake melted into their celluloid world.

● ● ●

They were outside the show and halfway down the
block when Tretheway realized he didn't have his
bowler. He stopped.

"Where's my hat?"

"What?" Jake stopped.

"My bowler. I don't have it."

"Did you have it when we left the show?"

Tretheway thought for a moment. "Damn. I
must've left it on the seat."

Neither spoke right away. A fresh wind whistled
around them. Jake knew what was coming.

"Just nip back there and see if they've found it,"
Tretheway said.

Jake trotted back to the theatre muttering to himself about why he was always the one that had to nip
back. When he re-emerged ten minutes later, Tretheway was nowhere in sight. Other pedestrians tramped
briskly toward their warm hearths. Jake looked both
ways. Tretheway stepped out of the darkened beauty
parlour doorway where he had taken refuge from the
chill. He'd wrapped his silk scarf over his head and
tied it under his double chins. Jake thought he resembled a very large, nineteenth-century peasant
woman.

"Did you get it?" Tretheway asked.

"No. They can't find it."

"What do you mean they can't find it?"

"They're still looking. Probably rolled under the
seats."

"With the candy?"

"I guess so."

Tretheway shook his head. "My favourite hat."

"It'll turn up somewhere." Jake's words were pro-phetic.

They trudged home in silence. Tretheway sulked. Visions of Addie's hot chocolate danced in Jake's head.

Chapter

2

Life carried on for the next few weeks just about the way it always did in Fort York, despite ominous war clouds gathering on the other side of the world. People who lived in the long shadows of such events tended to shift their worries to more mundane matters: ice falling dangerously close to shoppers from the city hall roof or the lopsided trimming of stately elms and maples on Aberdeen Avenue. Or they sought escape. Books worked. Vicarious radio adventures helped. But nothing transported anyone quicker or more effectively in time and place than the motion picture.

During the rest of the month, Tretheway and Jake were distracted from the real world by movies that included *Bulldog Drummond In Africa, Brother Rat, If I Were King, Ninotchka, Alexander's Ragtime Band, Girls On Probation* and *Goodbye Mr Chips.* On January 29, a Sunday, about twelve feature films since *Flying Deuces*, Tretheway received an unusual phone call. Or at least Addie did.

"That was Mrs Whiteside," Addie announced. She crossed the parlour to her half of the settee.

"Who?" Jake shared the maroon love seat with Addie. He had been twiddling the dial searching for the "Chase and Sanborn Hour" which, according to the FY Expo radio log, was supposed to follow the Jello program featuring Jack Benny. Tretheway half reclined in his oversized easy chair, reading the newspaper.

A small but adequate fire crackled in the fireplace. Light from its flames flickered along the dark body of Fred, the misnamed neighbour's dog, stretched out on the hearth. She was staying overnight. Shadows from the fringed lamps writhed on the walls. If you listened carefully, you could hear the winter wind dodging through the tall pines in the front yard. Everyone was sipping tea.

"You remember Mrs Whiteside," Addie continued. "A nice refined neighbour lady. Wouldn't hurt a fly. A widow. Her husband was killed about a year ago."

"I remember that." Jake found his radio program. The mellifluous voice of Don Ameche filled the room. Jake turned the volume down. "Wasn't it a plane crash?"

"That's right," Addie said. "He went down over Lake Ontario. They never found him." She looked at her brother. "You remember Albert?"

Tretheway grunted. He was reading a *FY Expo* pessimistic news item about the imminent fall of Barcelona.

"What did she want, Addie?" Jake asked.

"She just received a troublesome phone call."

"Oh?"

"The voice said, among other things, 'Your husband's in the garage.'"

"But I thought he was dead."

"He is."

Tretheway stirred. "Why didn't she call the police?" he said from behind his paper.

"She did in a way," Addie hedged. "I said you and Jake might . . ."

"Addie." Tretheway put his paper down. "I meant the police station. I don't make house calls."

"But it's so close by," Addie persisted.

"What did she find in the garage?" Jake asked.

"The poor soul's too afraid to look."

Tretheway pushed himself upright. "So you expect me to leave a warm room, on a good radio night, go out in the middle of winter . . ."

"Albert, she's my friend."

"All right, all right." Tretheway gulped down his tea. "Tell her we're on our way."

Addie refilled her own cup. "She's expecting you."

Tretheway glared at his sister.

"I'll get the coats." Jake jumped up from the settee.

● ● ●

Old, hard-packed snow covered the roads. The temperature had not strayed above freezing for two weeks and the wind, so comforting to hear when one was in front of a hospitable fire, became an enemy outdoors. Jake's toque, mitt and muffler set served him well but

Tretheway found it necessary to cup his gloved hands over his ears now and then because his donegal tweed peak cap, even pulled low, left his ear lobes unprotected. He'd never found his bowler

The walk through the deserted streets took a good fifteen minutes. Addie used the word neighbour loosely. Mrs Whiteside lived five long blocks away.

"I think this is the house," Jake said. "That must be Mrs Whiteside." He pointed to a stooped, apprehensive shadow peering through the sheer curtains of the front window. Mrs Whiteside had the door open before they had climbed the verandah steps. Wind chimes jingled overhead. Tretheway and Jake pushed gratefully into the warm hall.

"We'll leave our coats on, Mrs Whiteside." Tretheway removed his cap. "Just tell us about the phone call."

Mrs Whiteside spoke quietly. "It was a man, I think." Her brow wrinkled. She crossed her arms underneath a black cashmere cardigan that hung over her narrow shoulders. "He asked me if I believe in reincarnation."

"Reincarnation?" Tretheway repeated.

Mrs Whiteside nodded. "I thought it was some sort of religious call. So I said, 'I don't answer questions like that over the telephone.'"

"Quite right," Jake

"Then the voice said . . ." Mrs Whiteside hesitated. ". . . what I told Addie."

"Which was?" Tretheway prompted.

Mrs Whiteside looked out the window. Jake followed her gaze nervously.

"'Your husband is in the garage.'"

Outside the chimes continued their wind song.

"Mrs Whiteside." Tretheway paused. "I don't want to bring up any unpleasant memories, but wasn't your husband killed about a year ago?"

"Yes. He was." Her eyes filled. "A plane crash. In the lake."

"Could he still be alive?"

"No. Everyone agreed. The Coast Guard. All the rescue people. The insurance company." She took a deep breath. "He went down with his aircraft."

"Yet nobody ever found him?"

"No." Her brow wrinkled again.

"One more thing," Tretheway went on. "Do you have a car?"

"No. I sold it after my husband . . ."

"Then the garage is empty?"

"Yes. Except for the usual odds and ends. Garden tools, garbage cans, pots. And my bicycle."

Jake smiled. He remembered wondering how anyone could ride such an old black clunker around the neighbourhood and still look so elegant.

"We'll take it from here," Tretheway said. "I'm sure it's just a prank. A sick prank. There's a lot of funny people out there." He clapped his cap back on. "Let's go, Jake."

"I do appreciate you coming over like this," Mrs Whiteside said.

"Don't worry," Jake said. He held the door open for Tretheway, then followed his boss into the cold night.

● ● ●

The garage, separated from the house by a line of cedars, stood by itself at the rear of the lot. Tretheway strode purposefully up the driveway. Jake lagged behind.

"There's been a certain amount of traffic here," Tretheway said. He stopped and pointed at the pattern of ruts and footprints in the old snow. Jake caught up.

"Probably delivery vehicles," Tretheway said.

"Maybe a coal truck," Jake suggested.

Tretheway nodded. He resumed his stride.

"Shouldn't we have something?" Jake asked.

"What do you mean?"

"Like a revolver?"

"What?"

"Or even a stick?"

"Here." Tretheway took a long flashlight from his overcoat pocket. "Take this if it makes you feel any better."

Jake grumbled, but took it.

They stopped in front of the wooden garage doors.

"Did you hear that?" Jake asked. Tretheway shook his head.

They both listened.

A lone aircraft droned overhead. Car wheels whined in an icy rut blocks away. In a nearby yard two cats yowled over territory. Then a noise came from definitely inside the garage; metal dragging over concrete, several harsh metallic clanks, followed by something that could only be described as a snort.

"If I didn't know any better . . ." Tretheway swung the doors open.

A large, whinnying dapple-grey horse broke from the garage. Its huge shoulders brushed Tretheway roughly aside and knocked Jake off his feet into a snow-drift. Tretheway recovered first.

"Grab her!" he shouted.

"Me?" Jake pushed himself out of the snow. "Horses don't like me."

"Damn." Tretheway started down the driveway. As a former cavalry man, he found it hard to understand anyone's fear, ignorance or dislike of these noble beasts. He caught up to the horse at the edge of the street where she had stopped, reins dragging, as though waiting for him.

"There, there," Tretheway soothed. He picked up the reins carefully. "What the hell?" he said suddenly.

Jake, close behind, saw it at the same time. "What is it?" He turned the flashlight on.

"Don't spook her," Tretheway said.

Jake shut the light off. But not before the two of them had seen the hat fastened firmly on the horse's head: a bowler, at a rakish angle.

"Easy girl." Tretheway gently slid the wide elastic from under the horse's neck and removed the hat. The horse shook her head, relieved, Tretheway imagined, of the indignity. He hefted the bowler thoughtfully.

"You're not thinking what I'm thinking?" Jake asked.

"Hardly," Tretheway said. "How could it be mine?"

"You're right," Jake agreed. "They all look alike."

Tretheway flipped the hat over. Jake turned the flash on again, careful not to shine it in the horse's eyes. The beam of light illuminated clearly the gum drop stains on the bowler's white satin lining.

"What's going on?" Jake looked at his boss.

Tretheway shook his head. "I don't know."

"But who . . ."

"Go back to the Whitesides'," Tretheway ordered. "Tell her what happened. Call Central. See if anyone's reported something unusual. Like a stolen horse."

"Right." Jake pushed through the evergreens, scattering snow on his way to the house.

"Jake," Tretheway called after him. Jake stopped.

Tretheway held the bowler up. "My hat. Let's just keep this between you and me."

"Gotcha." Jake touched his forehead with the flashlight.

●　　●　　●

By the time Jake got back with some information, Tretheway had walked the horse back up the driveway into the protection of the garage. He had thrown his greatcoat over the animal's back and rump. The thought crossed Jake's mind that the horse was lucky to have been found by someone as large as Tretheway.

"Well?" Tretheway stood next to the steaming horse, basking in the amazing amount of heat the animal gave off. The garage was almost warm.

"There was a call about a stolen horse," Jake reported. "Two, three hours ago. From the Royal Oak Dairy. They've got a small farm and barn not too far from here. Over on the highway." Jake pointed south.

Tretheway nodded. "I know the place."

"Apparently the driver left the horse alone for a moment while he put the wagon away. After his milk deliveries. When he came back, the horse was gone."

"Wasn't he surprised?" Tretheway asked. "I mean, surely this doesn't happen every day?"

"Yes, he was," Jake said. "But not as much as you think. According to the dairy, it's not the first horse they've had stolen. But the time of year is unusual."

"Oh?"

"This is the first one in mid-winter. They've had several horses stolen, or borrowed they say, in the fall. When FYU starts its school year. They've never had one injured. And they're always returned or found soon after. Initiation? High spirits? Maybe. But not really criminal."

Tretheway fumbled in his pockets for a cigar, then remembered they were in his greatcoat pocket. He pointed to the shelf where his bowler lay. "Anything about the . . . ?"

Jake shook his head. Hooves clip-clopped on the cement floor as the horse shifted its weight. Jake backed off.

"Easy, easy." The horse nuzzled Tretheway. "She won't hurt you."

Jake looked unconvinced.

"Nice warm smell, isn't it?" Tretheway said.

Jake wrinkled his nose. "I called the dairy. They're sending a trailer over."

"What's her name?" Tretheway asked.

"Whose name?"

"The horse."

"I didn't ask."

Tretheway shook his head.

●　●　●

Back at the boarding house, Tretheway consoled himself with a quart of Blue. He had missed *Hollywood Playhouse, Grand Central Station* and half of the late news. Addie had waited up for them. When they told her the horse story (minus the part about Tretheway's bowler), she found it hard to believe, but was more concerned with her friend's well being.

"You're sure Mrs Whiteside's all right?" she asked.

Tretheway and Jake nodded.

"Good." She packed her knitting away. "Now I can go to bed."

"Good night, Addie," Jake said.

"Albert." Addie stopped by the hall closet. "There's an odour about your coat."

Tretheway smiled. "Pure horse, Addie."

She cluck-clucked her way down the hall. Tretheway puffed on his cigar. He waited until Addie could be heard going up the stairs before speaking.

"Does this horse episode remind you of anything?"

"Like what?"

"A movie."

"Could you be more specific?"

"What does *Flying Deuces* bring to mind?"

"A soft shoe."

"What?"

"Remember when they sang 'Shine On Harvest Moon'?" Jake explained. "How they danced? Fred Astaire's great, but when Stan and Ollie break into a soft shoe routine there's no one . . ."

"Never mind that. What about the ending?"

"Eh?" Jake paused. "Let me think. The Foreign Legion, the wild flying sequence, the crash. Then Ollie going up to heaven. A little corny maybe . . ." His eyes grew into saucers. "A horse. Then Ollie turns into a horse." He jumped up. "With a derby on!"

Tretheway waited for Jake to calm down before he went on. "And remember they discussed reincarnation earlier in the movie?"

"That's right." Jake sat down. "Ollie said he wanted to come back as a horse."

"Doesn't that remind you of tonight? A plane crash? With the pilot killed? Reincarnation? A horse with a derby?"

"Just about bang on." Jake's eyes were not returning to their normal size. "But what's it mean?"

"Probably nothing." Tretheway pushed himself out of the easy chair. He flipped his cigar into the fireplace. "Just a dumb student prank. Inspired by a silly movie."

Jake followed him down the hall. He watched while Tretheway took another beer out of the ice box and lowered himself gingerly onto the front edge of a kitchen chair. He stared across the room.

"So how come you're worried?" Jake said.

Tretheway took a long pull from the fresh quart.

"There are lots of things out there I can't figure out," he began. "Like Adolph Hitler's behaviour. Or Chamberlain's. Or even Roosevelt's. The war in Spain. Japan ravaging China. IRA bombings. But that's big stuff. I can't do much about it. And you like to think somebody else is keeping an eye on things." He turned and glowered at Jake. "But a few hours ago, only five blocks from my house, a nice widow lady is scared out of her bloomers by a sick phone call. Someone steals a horse and hides it in her garage. With my bowler on its head. Just like the movie. Coincidence? A prank? The start of something? I don't know. And it bothers me that I can't figure it out. That's why I'm worried."

Tretheway cradled his beer in one arm and clumped down the cellar steps to perform the nightly cold weather ritual of furnace stoking. Jake stood by himself in the kitchen. He listened absently to the muffled noises reverberating up through the network of old pipes and hot air ducts as Tretheway hurled shovelfuls of coal into the insatiable innards of the grey metal monster.

The twin vertical creases between Jake's eyebrows deepened. When Tretheway worried, he worried.

Chapter

3

The parade of movies continued into February. Tretheway and Jake saw such beauties as *Drums, Count of Monte Cristo, Dawn Patrol* and *You Can't Cheat An Honest Man* while enduring others best seen once and forgotten. This category included *Boy Meets Girl, The Devil Is Driving, Men Are Such Fools* and *Hold That Coed*.

Usually just Tretheway and Jake went together, but there were exceptions. Addie went to *Rebecca Of Sunnybrook Farm*. Tretheway passed. Bartholemew Gum joined them for *Gaiety Girls* and, a week later, *Blondie*. Jake saw them all.

Bartholemew Gum played cards regularly at the Tretheways' well known Saturday night euchre sessions. He lived with his mother only a few blocks away on the periphery of Coote's Paradise, a wildlife area protected in perpetuity by the Royal Fort York Botanical Gardens Society. As children, both Gum and Jake had roamed its two thousand acres of natural parks, forests, ravine trails and, depending on the season, canoed or skated on its marshy expanses. Active in the scout movement, Scouter Gum led his troops on hikes to destinations in Coote's with the evocative names of Kingfisher Point, Ginger Valley, Rat Island, Sassafrass Point and the Desjardins Canal. His colourless eyes gazed kindly at birds, animals and life through thick rimless glasses he had worn forever. He walked slowly, carefully looking down as though avoiding insects. What hair he had was curly.

Bartholemew Gum accompanied Tretheway and Jake to the showing of *Only Angels Have Wings.*

During the month several things happened that were to cause Tretheway some concern. On Sunday the eighteenth, in the late evening, a phone call verging on hysteria came into Central. A lady living in the area of Dundurn Castle reported a bird, a very large bird, sitting on a sturdy branch of an apple tree only feet from her rear window.

"I've seen smaller *people,*" she exclaimed.

The police calmed her down. They asked for a description. When the caller came back to the phone, she had to admit, with a touch of embarrassment, that the bird had flown. The police were naturally skeptical. Even the caller began to doubt her sighting. They didn't send a car.

The next call was different.

"Could you describe the bird?" the policeman asked.

"Big. Black. Some white on the wings. Skinny neck. His head looks bald and orange. White bill. His legs are pink. Eyes red."

"You're sure about this, sir?"

"He's sitting on my back porch," the gruff voice continued. "Under the verandah light. He's growling at me like a dog. We're eye to eye."

"What?"

"The son of a bitch is four feet tall."

The police sent a car.

Three burly policemen, aided by two SPCA employees hastily called in for the occasion, eventually cornered the disoriented bird in one of the small backyards. The amazed captors watched while the creature spread its wings, almost ten feet across, and attempted an awkward escape. It half flew into a fence and a tree, then rammed a storage shed in the next yard. Even though it was stunned, it took all of them to hold the bird's wings down and slip a small sack over the upper part of its body. A convenient but puzzling length of stout rope already tied to the bird's left ankle was used to bind its legs together. The SPCA pair carried the subdued bird to the waiting ambulance for the trip back to the shelter, an end to the night's entertainment. An early phone call to the police from Dundurn Castle the next day explained the whole thing, almost.

● ● ●

In 1832, Allan Napier McNab purchased property in Fort York's north-west end with a breathtaking view of Wellington Square Bay. Immediately the young lawyer began construction of a regency-style mansion that was to be, in his words, "the finest home west of Montreal." McNab named it Dundurn after his ancestral seat in Scotland. Impressed with its grandeur, the locals dubbed it a castle. The misnomer stuck.

Dundurn Castle contained about fifty rooms. They included an imposing entrance hall with a magnificent hanging walnut staircase, an elegant drawing room, a library, several sitting rooms, a smoking room and a formal grand dining room with French doors leading onto terraces and gardens. It also boasted a schoolroom for McNab's daughters.

Sir Allan McNab, knighted for his actions in the 1873 Rebellion, went on to great political success. He became in turn the leader of the Tory-Conservatives, Speaker of the Assembly and, from 1845 to 1856, the Prime Minister of Canada. During this period several additions were made to Dundurn; a family burial plot, stables, two elaborate gazebos, a small octagonal building to house cockfights and, of course, the customary aviary.

Such an estate demanded a lavish lifestyle, which in the end proved too expensive even for Sir Allan. At his death, Dundurn was heavily mortgaged. The furnishings were sold at auction and for two years it stood vacant. Subsequent residents also found it too costly to maintain. In 1900 the City of Fort York purchased the whole property and renamed it Dundurn Museum. It became a storehouse for artifacts and old furniture donated by well-meaning citizens. The locals still called it Dundurn Castle.

● ● ●

When the Museum staff reported for work that Monday morning, they discovered the damage. A heavy wire screen covering the outside section of the aviary had been cut and rolled back, providing easy access to the open skies for all the birds. This included their prize ornithologic exhibit, the California Condor.

As a possible compensation for being scared out of their wits the night before by an intimidating vulture, the people who lived in the neighbourhood of Dundurn awoke to a birdwatcher's bonanza. Grey and white cockatiels, tropical love birds, pheasant peacocks, South American cardinals, Peking robins and Zebra finches flitted as birds of a feather through trees and bushes or came to rest on porch railings and bird baths. During the next couple of days, some were humanely trapped by the SPCA or local birders and brought back, while a few, unused to freedom, returned on their own. Others fell prey to cats, hawks, freezing weather or simply flew to the horizon. By week's end, most of the birds, including the star condor, were safely back inside the repaired aviary.

The police classified it as a malicious prank and spent minimum time on the investigation. Citizens in the area and those who read about it in the *FY Expositor* tut-tutted over another case of senseless vandalism and went on to other things. Not so Tretheway.

● ● ●

"I don't like this Dundurn Castle thing either," Tretheway said.

"Either?" Wan Ho asked. "There's another one?"

"The stolen horse last month." Tretheway nodded at Jake. "Jake can explain."

"Well . . ." Jake looked at his boss.

"Go ahead." Tretheway prepared himself for a brief embarrassment. "Tell him the whole story. Including the bowler."

As Sergeant of Detectives, Wan Ho had scanned the stolen horse report. He had not, however, heard about Tretheway's and Jake's part.

Wan Ho played euchre regularly at the Tretheways'. From time to time he joined Tretheway and Jake on movie nights, particularly if a Charlie Chan was on the bill. He and Jake were familiar with all the Honolulu detective's many aphorisms.

Charles Wan Ho had been born in Canada to Chinese parents. His oriental features, refuting ancient Far Eastern legends, usually reflected his emotions; in his own words, not inscrutable. Wan Ho had barely made the minimum height and weight requirements for the police force, but more than made up for this by moving and thinking more quickly than his occidental colleagues. He had risen rapidly throughout the ranks to the impasse of sergeant. In Tretheway's opinion, the FYPD was lucky to have him as a detective.

It was the end of the week. Tretheway had asked Wan Ho to the house ostensibly for some Saturday night euchre, but in truth he was worried about the condor episode. It bothered him for the same reason the stolen horse bothered him; no explanation to scratch the itch of his curiosity. He wanted to talk. The three were sipping hot tea in Addie's kitchen before the card game started. Tretheway sat by while Jake brought Wan Ho

up to date on the bowler saga. He suffered their sup-
pressed mirth in silence.

"How come *your* hat?" Wan Ho asked finally.

"Dumb luck on his part," Tretheway said. "He
must've somehow come across the hat after he'd seen
Flying Deuces. Fit right in with the movie. Triggered a
plan in his mind. A good starter." He blew on his tea.
"In any case he, or for that matter she, was in the theatre. And for the sake of argument, let's assume our
very own West End. Let's see." Tretheway looked at
Jake. "We saw *Flying Deuces* on Monday." Jake nodded. "That means whoever found the hat probably saw
the movie on Monday also."

"It ran for three days," Wan Ho reminded him.

"The hat could've been stuck under a seat for a
night or two," Jake said.

Tretheway reconsidered. "You're right." He
drained his tea cup. It was twice the size of anyone
else's. "So let's say this joker took my hat and saw *Flying Deuces* on the Monday, Tuesday or Wednesday."

Jake and Wan Ho nodded in agreement.

"But we still don't know why," Jake said.

"No," Tretheway said. "But I'm going to find out."

Neither Jake nor Wan Ho envied the bowler thief.

"But back to this condor thing," Tretheway said.

"You think it's related to the stolen horse?" Wan
Ho asked.

"I don't know that either," Tretheway said. "Just a
feeling. It seems more than random violence. With no
purpose. For one thing, whoever did it had to bring
heavy wire cutters."

"You keep saying condor," Jake said. "Why? What
about all the other birds?"

"The rope," Tretheway explained. "The rope on the condor's leg. As though someone tried to hobble the bird beforehand."

"Like the SPCA men eventually did," Jake remembered.

"With the help of three or four uniforms, don't forget," Wan Ho said.

"Which suggests why our vandal was unsuccessful," Tretheway said.

"He worked by himself?" Jake asked.

Tretheway nodded. "Or herself."

Jake and Wan Ho took a moment to digest this food for thought.

Tretheway spoke to Wan Ho. "Now we need your help."

"Mine?" Wan Ho said. "In what way?"

"You have access to all the reports and information received in the detective division." It was a statement, not a question.

"That's right."

"If I want to see them, I have to make an official point of it. You know Zulp."

Wan Ho and Jake both grinned at Tretheway's reference to their leader Horace Zulp, an old-line policeman from a time when long service meant more than competence, who had simply outlasted his competition to become Chief Constable. His career was framed with uncrossable boundaries. Beat constables walk the beat. Detectives investigate. Cadets do what they're told. And traffic police handle traffic.

"You want to know about stop signs or crosswalks?" Jake said. "We're your man."

Tretheway smiled briefly and got back to business. "What I want to know is if anything unusual happened around that time. Mid-February. Think about it."

Wan Ho stared into his cup as if he were reading the tea leaves for a long, quiet fifteen seconds before answering. "Nothing springs to mind."

"Something you can't explain," Tretheway prodded.

Wan Ho went quiet again. "Nothing important."

"But there was something?"

"I don't see how it could relate."

"Try me."

"A prowler." Wan Ho took a notebook from his inside pocket. He leafed through it and stopped. "Last Wednesday. The fifteenth. A prowler was reported. Again on Thursday and Friday. Three separate complaints. Three consecutive nights."

"The same one?" Tretheway asked.

"We don't know. Never caught him."

"What'd he look like?" Tretheway asked.

"Man or woman?" Jake asked.

"A shadowy figure lurking in the bushes," Wan Ho read.

"But still just a prowler," Tretheway said.

"Except for the complainants' name." Wan Ho checked his note book again. "Dabb. D-A-B-B. Last name of Dabb."

"Which one?" Tretheway asked.

"All of them."

"Eh?"

"They all had the same name."

"Were they related?" Tretheway asked.

Wan Ho shook his head. "Nope. They didn't even know each other. All from different parts of the city."

Tretheway leaned against the protesting back of his chair. He folded his arms across his chest as far as they would go. "Doesn't that stretch the laws of coincidence?"

"I'd say so," Jake said.

Wan Ho shrugged.

The swinging doors of the kitchen flew open as Addie pushed through. "Euchre time, gentlemen."

● ● ●

For the next couple of hours cards prevailed. They played in the sizable common room next to the kitchen. On a card table in the middle of the room stood two thin euchre decks, counters, a deep dish of peanuts, a glass of beer each for Wan Ho and Jake and Tretheway's mandatory quart bottle. A small crystal flute of dandelion wine marked Addie's place. Three matching bridge chairs plus Tretheway's substantial wooden special, which Addie had bought at a farm auction and slipcovered with her own brightly coloured crocheting, surrounded the table. An occasional student boarder passed through, exchanging pleasantries with the card players, on his way to the kitchen. The students generally had free rein in tea- and sandwich-making as long as they cleaned up after themselves. Two of them sat now on one of the common room's cushiony chairs perusing text books and term papers. A third rose when necessary to change records on the victrola. Sounds of Mozart, Paul Whiteman, Benny

Goodman or, Jake's favourite, Duke softly intruded by turns. Fred the Labrador sat on the hearth facing the action. Behind her the fire crackled comfortingly in the red brick fireplace, reminding everyone that, although the weather outside appeared still and clear, the temperature still hugged zero on this last day in February.

"Albert," Addie said. "You just trumped your partner's ace."

"What?"

"Your trump." Addie pointed to the offending black spot on Jake's red virgin ace.

"Sorry." Tretheway retrieved his card and followed suit.

"Now it's my turn." Addie trumped the ace and pulled the cards into her neat pile of tricks. "That's a euchre. And game."

Jake frowned.

"Good play, Addie," Wan Ho said, gathering all the cards together. He couldn't stop smiling. "My deal." He and Addie were well ahead of the resident champions in games and rubbers.

"You're not playing with your usual fervour," Addie said. What she meant was that Tretheway hadn't been smacking his aces or bowers enthusiastically onto the green felt table top, threatening its stability. "Are you okay?"

"I'm just fine, Addie." Tretheway smiled, lips only. "Just got things on my mind."

Jake and Wan Ho exchanged glances.

It had been one of those evenings. Tretheway had not played his customary aggressive game. He hadn't even criticized Jake on a couple of improper leads. And although someone had made sure a Blue was always within reach, he hadn't actually asked for it. They played two more fast games that he and Jake lost.

"Maybe we should call it a night," Tretheway suggested.

"Oh, no, you don't." Wan Ho eagerly stacked the cards into a pile and pushed them towards Addie. "Your deal, partner." A wide toothy grin split his face. "Take no prisoners."

Tretheway sat back resignedly. He half closed his eyes and dreamily listened to the hypnotic repetition of Addie's shuffle. A log in the fire popped. Strains of "Mood Indigo" flowed from the victrola. Fred sighed noticeably. Outside a fresh breeze wafted several brittle leftover maple leaves against the glass of the French doors. The sound of a low flying airplane buzzed clearly through the frosty night air.

Tretheway blinked; not a delicate, tear-cleansing flick but a snapping, close-to-audible cartoon click. His eyes flashed.

"That's it." Tretheway straightened up. His fist whacked the centre of the card table. The peanuts jumped upwards. Jake, alerted in time by the blur of his boss's arm, steadied the beer glasses. The students stopped talking. Fred barked.

"Albert!" Addie protested, hugging her wine glass to her chest.

"You know what our trouble is?" Tretheway glared around the table.

Jake and Wan Ho shook their heads.

"We see too many movies."

"You could cut down," Addie said.

"No, no. I mean it's hard to remember them all."

"What are you driving at?" Wan Ho said.

"About three weeks ago we saw *Only Angels Have Wings*." Tretheway pointed to the sky. "About flying. In South America. The Andes. If you remember, in one scene a giant bird . . ."

"A condor." Jake came to life.

"Crashed through the windshield of Thomas Mitchell's plane," Tretheway finished.

"I didn't see that one," Wan Ho said.

"I remember it," Jake said. "The co-pilot landed the plane. But Thomas Mitchell died."

"Broke his neck," Tretheway said.

"Maybe I'll get the sandwiches," Addie said. She left the table.

"You feel there's a connection between the movie and the Dundurn aviary thing?" Wan Ho asked.

"Yes," Tretheway said.

"You're still guessing, though," Wan Ho said.

"There's more," Tretheway said.

The students left the room. Fred settled down. Tretheway leaned back in his chair again and reached for a cigar. Jake struck a wooden match and held it up in front of his boss. Tretheway made a small ceremony of puffing life into the White Owl.

"Sometimes it takes longer than other times to happen." His large hand waved away the excessive smoke. "But if you're patient, push the clouds away, let a little light in, eventually . . ." Tretheway smiled at his two listeners. "Thomas Mitchell played the part of a man called Dabb. Kid Dabb."

"The prowler," Wan Ho said.

"Prowlee," Jake corrected.

"Let me take you all the way down the path."

Tretheway listened for a moment to Addie slamming cupboard doors in the kitchen before he went on. "I say our perpetrator, let's call him or her the Fan, saw *Flying Deuces*, got an idea, found my hat, stole a horse and did his trick."

Jake and Wan Ho nodded.

"Then a few weeks later he saw *Only Angels Have Wings*, became inspired again. Decided to recreate Thomas Mitchell's or Dabb's scene." Tretheway picked up some of the peanuts that had jumped onto the table and popped them into his mouth. "So what's the first thing he'd do?"

"Get a condor," Jake said.

"No," Wan Ho said. "He'd look for a Dabb."

"Right," Tretheway said. "He'd have to decide what to do with the bird first. So he reconnoitered all the Dabbs." He looked at Wan Ho. "Not a common name?"

"Only three in the phone book," Wan Ho said.

"So he had to choose the one that best suited his purposes," Tretheway continued. "Check the layout of the house and grounds. Make sure there is a Mr Dabb living there. And anything else he might stumble across." He took a long puff of his cigar. "What I like to call 'accidental technique.'"

Jake and Wan Ho waited.

"One of the Dabbses might be called Kid. Or look like Thomas Mitchell. Or be a pilot. Or even be from South America," Tretheway explained. "But it doesn't matter. Because the capture of the condor didn't come off."

"So this was not vandalism?" Wan Ho asked. "This was a plot to steal the condor?"

"Nothing to do with the other birds?" Jake added.

"Right." Tretheway answered them both.

"But what was he going to do with the condor?" Jake asked.

"We'll never know," Tretheway said. "Maybe throw the bird through his living room window. Or the car windshield. Maybe just leave him in the garage like the horse. But, once again, it doesn't matter. Our illustrious Fan aborted number two. Let's wait for number three."

"Number three?" Wan Ho said.

"You mean . . . ?" Jake began.

The kitchen door swung open. "Sandwiches, Gentlemen." Addie swept through, carrying a large circular tray laden with three-year-old cheddar cheese sandwiches; not the two-bite, triangular, green-dyed cocktail specimens, but solid, two-handed specials made with thick slices of whole wheat bread that she had baked the same morning. A dish of strong onions and pickles stood on the side. Addie stopped abruptly. "I mean, unless you're still talking shop."

"No, Addie," Tretheway said. "We're all finished."

Addie put the heavy tray in the centre of the card table. Everyone dug in. Two students returned and split one sandwich. Fred had half of Jake's. Addie and Wan Ho enjoyed their share, but Tretheway ate more than anyone. In his hands, the sandwiches appeared regular sized. The tray emptied quickly.

Tretheway brushed the last bread crumbs from his chest onto his stomach. "Now let's play some real cards," he said.

"But you said . . ." Addie began.

"I think it's your deal," Tretheway said.

Addie started shuffling the cards. She frowned across the table at Wan Ho.

"Jake," Tretheway said. "Just nip out to the kitchen and get me a brew."

Jake pushed away from the table. He smiled. Tretheway was back in the game.

● ● ●

At the end of the evening, Tretheway walked Wan Ho to the front door while Jake and Addie attacked the post-euchre clutter of the common room. Wan Ho was mumbling to himself; phrases like 'bad run of cards', 'lucky splits'. He and Addie had lost five quick consecutive games with Tretheway holding four lone hands.

"There'll be another day," Tretheway said. He helped the grumbling detective on with his coat.

Wan Ho pushed his feet into an open pair of galoshes. He looked around at Tretheway. The muted bantering of Jake and Addie floated down the hall.

"You said something about number three," Wan Ho said.

Tretheway nodded.

"You think there'll be another one?"

"Maybe not. It's hard to tell. One is just an event. Two could be a coincidence. But three changes the picture. That's a series. A pattern."

"Meaning?"

"That there could eventually be a number four. And a five. Six. And so on."

Wan Ho pulled on his gloves. "Anything we can do about it?"

"I think not. It depends on which movie our Fan sees. And if it gives him an idea. As I said before, there are just too many movies. If he can find a Laurel and Hardy sinister, then . . ." Tretheway shrugged.

Wan Ho nodded. "And really, a derby on a horse and an escaped bird are nothing to lose sleep over."

"That's right." Tretheway reached out and pulled the lapels of Wan Ho's overcoat snugly together. "As far as I'm concerned, they're just two interesting but petty unrelated incidents."

"Not a series?" Wan Ho smiled.

"Not a series." Tretheway smiled back. "See you at the movies." He opened the door. Arctic air rushed into the hall. They both shivered.

After *The Wizard of Oz* a pattern was formed, a series began.

Chapter

One of the first things Tretheway did in 1937 when he became the youngest inspector (traffic or otherwise) on the FYPD was to organize a children's safety club. It started innocently enough. A first grade teacher from the local George R. Allan Public School approached Tretheway with the strong opinion that her pupils were not sufficiently aware of traffic rules and regulations. And could the police do anything about it.

Tretheway thought so. He began one slow Monday morning by giving her class of six-to-seven-year-olds a short talk on road safety. The school invited him back. Addie typed up membership cards. A student could join by filling out the card (no charge) and memorizing a half-dozen traffic safety rules. Addie also came up with the name "Little Shavers Road Protection Club" while Jake thought the words "Traffic Dodgers" should be included. Tretheway put his conservative foot down by christening the group simply "The Fort York Children's Safety Club." It caught on.

Tretheway spoke to other classes, then to the upper grades of George R. Allan. The club spread to other public schools in the city. It even found a receptive ear in the lower forms of the five high schools. The amount of public support amazed everyone. Short complimentary stories began appearing in the *FY Expositor*. Churches praised the club. The local radio station donated seven minutes of broadcasting time every school morning from 8:03 to 8:10 following the news. Tretheway, Wan Ho quipped, was thrust into show business.

The show's format was simple. Its main feature consisted of one basic traffic rule every day usually read by Tretheway in a voice that came out as stagey but believable. He also conducted pertinent interviews with crossing guards, ambulance drivers, firemen, motorcycle policemen and sometimes local celebrities like the FY Taggers football coach or Mayor Phineas "Fireball" Trutt. The program opened and closed with a transcription of Gracie Fields singing "Look to the Left and Look To The Right and You'll Never Never Get Run Over."

So when Freeman Thake offered the use of his West End theatre to the FY Children's Safety Club at half price (five cents a head) for a special Saturday matinee of *The Wizard of Oz*, Tretheway was not surprised at the turnout. They filled all 420 seats. The few brave mothers and fathers who turned up to supervise were not enough. But the staff pitched in.

Joshua Pike and Lulu Ashcroft ushered children to the bathrooms as well as their seats. Violet Farrago, after closing her ticket booth, shouted at unrulies running up and down the aisles. Freeman Thake himself did his urbane best, herding squealing groups to their destinations. Others volunteered.

Mayor Trutt, ever mindful of his political image, arrived with his wife Bertha to aid in the crowd control festivities. The glistening chain of office hung from his neck over his stout midsection. Thin coordinated arms and legs stuck out from his body. A shock of white hair topped his beet-red face and large matching nose. Rumours started by his detractors suggested his flamboyant colouring came from the drink. Kinder, more humourous critics said it was from standing too close to flames for too long. Mayor Trutt had in fact earned his nickname "Fireball" by serving for twenty years with the FY Fire Department before he stumbled into the political system. His relationship with fire still bordered on phobia.

Mrs. Trutt was the woman behind the man. The mayor had achieved his career success by following her advice. Bertha Trutt understood and enjoyed politics. As tall as her husband, a little plumper and a little heavier, she still radiated a charm envied by svelter ladies. She puffed constantly and unaffectedly on Player's cork tips through a long ebony cigarette holder. As the first lady of Fort York, her pleasant conversations and anecdotes enriched every important Fort York social function. Bertha and Addie had hit it off from their first meeting.

Addie had begged off the special matinee to prepare Saturday's dinner. Jake had brought Bartholemew Gum. Wan Ho had volunteered. And Doc Nooner attended in his professional capacity.

"What's one more group?" Doc had laughed when Tretheway asked him why he bothered.

Dr Francis Nooner served as MD for the police, the firemen, city council and the FY Taggers' football club as well as being the city coroner. His round naturally tonsured head sat atop a round overweight upper body with a round rear end below; all a result of his flagrant disregard for the rules of self-indulgence that he preached to others. Short stocky legs destroyed the illusion of a snowman. His deep booming contagious laugh could easily be heard above the many shrill voices of the audience.

Competent Nurse Lodestone stood tall and intimidating by the Doc's side. Her starched white uniform stretched across a torso that wouldn't have looked out of place on the prow of a Viking ship. She easily carried a large bag bulky with medical tape, salve, bandages, tongue depressors, aspirins and bottles of bright red mercurochrome.

Tretheway had asked Miles Terminus to give them a hand. He knew that since his mandatory retirement three years ago, time had hung heavy for the quiet spoken former policeman. Terminus had joined the force the same year as Zulp but lacked the Chief's ambition or luck for advancement. After nineteen years on the force, he had been promoted to First Class Constable; 1919, the year of the Vincent Paradiso incident.

One cool autumn night on Fort York's beach strip, a narrow piece of land separating Wellington Square Bay from Lake Ontario, Constable Terminus was patrolling a line of summer cottages, more than half of them empty. He heard glass breaking. Rounding the

corner of the nearest cottage, he surprised, then chal-
lenged an obvious burglar. The shadowy figure ad-
vanced toward Terminus, threatening the policeman
with a rifle. After another unheeded warning, the nine-
teen-year veteran fired his revolver. The .38 calibre
bullet, more by chance than skill, bore a neat, blood-
less hole between the eyes of the burglar. He dropped
his rifle. It turned out to be a hockey stick. Vincent
Paradiso, recidivist, second-storey man, pillar of the
criminal community was, at the time of his death, out
on bail pending an assault charge; hardly a model citi-
zen. Because of this, taking into account Terminus's
undistinguished but clean record, those in power ex-
onerated the policeman. But from that point on, his
career turned into a long wait for a pension. He saw
no more promotions. Terminus handled the affair well,
seldom spoke of it and seemed outwardly contented.
Although he spent the rest of his time at an inside desk
job, Terminus never lost the lumbering, big-footed gait
of a veteran beat policeman, albeit slower and less
strong in his later years. He visited the Tretheways'
regularly but seldom played euchre.

Each of Tretheway's supplementary volunteer
force stationed himself around the theatre to help in
any way he could. The enthusiastic shrieks of the
young audience stilled somewhat in anticipation when
the title and opening credits rolled by, rose to fervent
pitch when the tornado struck and changed to loud
oohs and aahs when the film switched to technicolour
as Dorothy entered the land of the Munchkins. From
the time the Wicked Witch of the East was crushed by
Dorothy's falling house to the scene where her sister,

the Wicked Witch of the West ('she's even worse than the other one'), was gruesomely liquidated, the decibel level varied from loud to screech. During relative lulls, singing scenes especially, excited club members ran up and down the aisles dodging slow-moving adult monitors and ignoring the cries of Violet Farrago. An endless stream of children going to the bathroom, usually walking backwards, added to the ambience. Few young eyes left the screen. And the Witch provoked the most screaming.

Just past the three-quarter mark, Tretheway, with Jake in tow, sneaked up to the second floor. They paused at the projection booth. Tretheway tapped on the glass panel in the door. He waved. Neil Heavenly mouthed a greeting and waved back. They proceeded to the crying room.

"I don't know how he does it," Tretheway said.

"Does what?" Jake asked.

"Sees the same movies over and over again."

"I wouldn't mind."

Tretheway shook his head.

At the end of the upper hall (no balcony) the company that orginally built the theatre had installed a crying room, so called because they thought mothers with crying babies could retire there and not disturb others. It contained two rows of extra wide seats, with ash trays. A pane of thick, soundproof glass separated the patrons from the common folk. Speakers carried the sound. More often the room hosted sympathy cases like people with canes, crutches, casts or hacking coughs. And sometimes friends of Thake trying to get away from it all.

"Well look who's here," Tretheway said.

"Too many kids." Wan Ho's grin was sheepish.

"Sneaky. Pretty sneaky," Jake said.

"That makes three of us." Wan Ho defended himself.

Tretheway settled comfortably into one of the seats. The heavy door eased shut, enveloping them in silence. Wan Ho had turned off the sound.

"Great movie," Jake said.

"Not really my cup of tea." Tretheway wriggled until he found a cigar.

"The kids sure love it," Jake said.

Wan Ho smiled at Tretheway. "At least we won't have to worry about this one."

"What do you mean?" Tretheway said.

"Surely our Fan won't see anything ominous in this movie."

"Why?" Tretheway pressed.

"It's just a kid's movie. A silly fairy tale. Not serious," Wan Ho said.

"You think *Flying Deuces* was an epic?" Tretheway said.

"Well . . ."

"You mean he might use *The Wizard of Oz*?" Jake said.

"All I'm saying is, keep an open mind." Tretheway puffed cigar smoke into the small room. Through the glass Frank Morgan recited a silent speech from his Omaha State Fair hot air balloon. "Put yourself in the Fan's place. What would he do?" Tretheway looked from Jake to Wan Ho. "How could he use this movie?"

"Okay." Wan Ho thought for a moment. "We need a death."

"Preferably violent," Jake said.

"Like in the first two movies."

"Like Dorothy killing the Witch. Liquidating her," Jake quoted.

"Maybe he's going to melt somebody," Wan Ho suggested.

Jake winced.

"I doubt that," Tretheway said. "But . . ." he shrugged.

Jake and Wan Ho continued their exchange.

"Don't forget," Wan Ho said. "The first witch was killed too."

"By a falling house," Jake said.

"How about death by tornado?"

"Or fire. Remember the scarecrow was set on fire."

"And in another scene he was torn apart."

"And the poppies."

"Eh?"

"The Witch tried to poison them all with the poppies. Put them to sleep."

"And how would you like to be dropped by one of those flying monkeys?"

Jake and Wan Ho looked at each other. Neither smiled.

"Just a silly fairy tale," Tretheway repeated.

"I shouldn't've said that," Wan Ho said.

"There's too many possibilities," Jake said.

"And too many movies," Tretheway said.

The three stared glumly through the glass. The movie had returned to black and white. Dorothy lay on her bed surrounded by family and friends. Her lips were moving. Wan Ho flicked on the speakers.

"Oh, Auntie Em. There's no place like home."

Chapter Four

Tretheway pushed himself out of the soft seat. "I couldn't agree more." He led Jake and Wan Ho out of the crying room.

Chapter

5

About three weeks later in the north end of Fort York, where light industry mixed freely with residences, a house was knocked flat; at least most of it was. It happened around three o'clock in the morning, April 1, a Saturday.

Abruptly awakened by an approaching roar, Isabella Hamilton, an elderly spinster, scrambled to safety seconds before a massive bulldozer tumbled the concrete block and stucco wall of her basement bedroom about her. She suffered understandable shock, but physically only some minor bruises from being grazed by falling debris. The FYPD inferred that the bulldozer had been stolen from a nearby construction company with sloppy security. Witnesses were hard to come by in this transitional neighbourhood where residents minded their own business. Miss Hamilton went on to say that when the dozer stopped, she heard a high-pitched voice, presumably the driver's singing. She didn't recognize the song but was sure it began with the words "Ding Dong."

● ● ●

That was enough for Tretheway. He hastily called an unofficial gathering of the professional show folk for the following Sunday. And because of their involvement in *The Wizard of Oz* screening, and the fact that Addie could use their help in logistics (refreshments and chairs), Tretheway invited Gum, Wan Ho, Doc Nooner and Miles Terminus. Nooner was the only one who couldn't make it. His Connoisseur Wine and Gourmet Hors D'Oeuvre Club met the first Sunday of each month. The rest of the guests took over the Tretheways' common room at eight in the evening.

Apple logs burned in the fireplace. Soft music came from Addie's kitchen radio. Fred sat beside one of the couches, her head on Jake's lap. An aura of contentment that would soon disappear pervaded the room.

Tretheway started slowly. He thanked them all for coming, especially on such short notice, and launched into a general, off-the-cuff dissertation on the importance of movies to small neighbourhood like West End. And about how they influenced some people more than others. His audience reacted politely enough, but most brows remained wrinkled. He followed with a brief, hit-the-high-spots retelling of *The Wizard of Oz*. He then jumped right in. He laid bare his theory connecting the movie to the bulldozer incident. Audible gasps came from Violet Farrago and Lulu Ashcroft when they realized what Tretheway was saying.

"You mean," Violet Farrago said, "that someone purposely tried to push the wall on top of that Miss Hamilton?"

"It's only a theory." Tretheway held both placating hands out in front of him, palms down, fingers spread. "But yes."

"But the paper said vandalism," Lulu said.

"I believe Chief Zulp's phrase was . . . ?" Tretheway looked at Wan Ho.

"'Extreme but spur of the moment vandalism,'" Wan Ho quoted.

"And you're saying, in your opinion, it's . . . it's . . ." Lulu couldn't say the word.

"Murder," Tretheway finished. "Fortunately only attempted. But still premeditated murder."

"Now just a minute, Inspector." Freeman Thake rose quietly from his seat. "If I understand, you're saying that someone saw *The Wizard of Oz*, saw Dorothy's house fall on the Witch and tried to emulate this?"

"That's right," Tretheway said.

"Come, come Inspector," Thake argued. "What about the bulldozer? You can't plan that?"

"True," Tretheway said. "But it is all part of his technique. His targets of opportunity approach. I'm convinced he planned something else. His own vehicle perhaps. I've seen the Hamilton home. Concrete blocks. Not too substantial. Wouldn't take much to knock it over. But when you're practically handed a bulldozer," Tretheway poked his stubby index finger in the air, "much more efficient. And spectacular." Thake sat down muttering.

"But what about the noise?" Violet asked.

"It's a noisy area," Tretheway said. "Close to Stelfy. Not too many homes." He mentioned that there were no witnesses. "Also, it's a tight-lipped neighbourhood."

Joshua Pike entered the discussion. "Just how do you explain the singing?" He stretched as tall as his short legs would allow. Both hands rested on the chair in front of him, taking the weight off his bunioned feet. From the waist up, he was a big man. His prominent teeth, set in a jutting lantern jaw, showed pleasantly as he spoke. "The song? The one that started 'Ding Dong'?"

"Remember the song the Munchkins sang in the movie?" Tretheway asked.

Joshua shook his large head.

"'Ding Dong, the Witch Is Dead,'" Tretheway reminded

Lulu and Violet inhaled loudly again.

"In the paper it said a high-pitched voice," Joshua said. "Does this suggest a woman was driving the bulldozer?"

"Maybe, maybe not," Tretheway said. "More likely an attempt by our Fan to imitate a Munchkin."

"Isn't that taxing the imagination just a bit?" Miles Terminus said. "Couldn't it still be a coincidence?"

"Too many coincidences, Miles," Tretheway said. "And I'll give you one more. The name of the woman almost killed by the falling house was Hamilton. The name of the actress who plays the Witch in the movie was also Hamilton. Margaret Hamilton."

"That could still be a coincidence," Lulu said.

"I agree," Thake said. "After all, it was just one movie. And just one . . . ah . . . misadventure."

Tretheway sighed. He shook his head. "No. This is the third. There were two other movies. And, as you say, misadventures."

Tretheway waited for the facts to sink in during the stunned lull that followed.

"I'll make some tea," Addie said. She left.

"I'll help," Gum said following Addie to the kitchen.

Tretheway went on to explain about *Flying Deuces* and *Only Angels Have Wings.*

"I can understand your surprise," he concluded. "The stolen horse and derby never made the paper. And the condor plan was aborted. You have not been privy to all the facts." He nodded at Jake and Wan Ho. "We have. The three incidents alone are mere stories. Even amusing. But in my opinion, connected together they foretell a pattern of escalating danger. Even murder."

They all resumed or re-arranged themselves in their seats. Chairs creaked. A kettle whistled in the kitchen. Neil Heavenly raised his hand.

"Yes, Neil," Tretheway said.

"There's one question nobody's asked," he said. "But I think it's important."

"I can guess what it is," Tretheway said. "But go ahead."

Neil Heavenly stood up. His curly, reddish brown forelock bounced boyishly on his freckled brow. He looked younger than twenty-seven. According to Thake, Neil had driven his battered pickup truck out of the depressed prairies about four years ago, heading for a more affluent Southern Ontario. He'd held a number of jobs, one of them as a projectionist. Thake hired him and had never regretted it. Although small in stature, Heavenly easily hefted the numerous un-wieldy cans of film and hopped nimbly around the complicated projector. He was habitually early on the job and usually the last to leave the theatre. His knowl-edge of cinematic history rivalled Jake's. He lived alone, lifted weights and bit his nails to the quick.

"Why?" Neil Heavenly asked. He pushed his hands self-consciously into his pockets. "Why is this person doing all these mysterious deeds?"

"That's the one," Tretheway said. "Good question. And I can give you a straightforward answer."

Jake and Wan Ho exchanged puzzled looks.

"I don't know," Tretheway said. "I have absolutely no idea why our Fan is doing what he's doing."

Lulu giggled nervously. Neil Heavenly sat down, his hands still in his pockets. China and cutlery noises came from the kitchen. Miles Terminus spoke.

"There's one thing we haven't determined."

"What's that, Miles?" Tretheway asked.

"Are you sure our Fan, as you call him, saw all the movies at the West End?"

"Good point," Tretheway said. "We spent a little time last week at the Expo office. Checking the movie ads from January on."

Jake smiled at the choice of "we."

"All three movies played at different theatres by themselves," Tretheway explained. "But only at the West End did they all play. Is that likely, Freeman?"

"Hard to tell without checking," Thake said. "But it's possible."

"Neil?" Tretheway asked.

Neil Heavenly nodded in agreement.

"So let's assume that our Fan is a West End regular," Tretheway said.

"But what about *The Wizard of Oz*?" Violet asked. "It was all children."

"We were all there," Joshua said.

"And other adults," Lulu said.

"That's right," Terminus said. "Parents."

"We're assuming they were parents," Wan Ho said.

"For that matter," Tretheway said, "anyone could've slipped in that day." He let the group simmer down before he went on. "Think about this for a moment. It's possible that Vi sold our Fan a ticket. That Freeman tore it in half. And Lulu or Joshua ushered him to a seat." Tretheway paused. "At least three times."

Chapter

6

April proved to be a wet month; the wettest in twenty-three years, the Fort York meteorologist said. And world events reflected the dismal local weather. Poland mobilized one million men. The Nazis openly boasted that the Allies could do nothing against Germany's might. Roosevelt said such talk was "a menace to world peace" indicating his support for England and France. And if that weren't enough, King Zog (a name reminiscent of someone from Oz, Tretheway thought) and his Queen Geraldine fled Albania ahead of Mussolini's army fanning one more ember in the smouldering fire of European events.

On the escape side, Hollywood plowed ahead with missiles good and bad such as, *Torchy Blane In Panama*, *Jezebel*, *Love Finds Andy Hardy*, *Algiers* (Addie went because of Hedy Lamarr's co-star, Charles Boyer), *Yellow Jack*, *Damaged Goods* ("the picture that dares to tell

the truth") and *In Old Chicago*. Addie also joined
Tretheway and Jake for *Bluebeard's Eighth Wife* with
Claudette Colbert and Gary Cooper, not because of the
stars or title, but because it was dish night.

Over a period of two years, Addie had collected
close to a service of eight pale yellow china with a central floral motif similar to the one woven into the West
End's lobby carpet. The theatre gave them away, piece
by piece, every other Wednesday as a bonus for at-
tending. At least once every dish night a plate or saucer got away and rolled down the cement floor between
the carpeted aisles and the seats, noisily gaining speed
until it shattered climactically against the proscenium
arch. The crowd customarily cheered. So did Tretheway and Jake. Addie didn't. She put that type of
behaviour in the same class as the public school boys
who smuggled plumber's friends into the theatre to
disrupt kissing scenes.

At different times Tretheway and Jake were accompanied by Wan Ho (*Charlie Chan at Treasure Island*),
Bartholemew Gum, Miles Terminus and once, when
Young Doctor Kildare was showing, Doc Nooner. The
movie that counted, the one that inspired the Fan,
though nobody knew it at the time, was screened on
Thursday, April 6. Wan Ho joined Tretheway and Jake
on that evening.

● ● ●

A steady light rain dogged the trio as they walked to
the movie house. Tretheway led the way, protected
from the elements by his rubber traffic slicker and wet
bowler. Jake and Wan Ho followed, huddled under

Jake's oversized golf umbrella. The first movie started sharp at seven.

An imposing statue of "Victoria Regina Imperatrix" stares haughtily from the screen. An invisible military band plays "God Save The Queen." The title appears on a huge gong accompanied by spritely Rudyard Kipling music and a deep voice stating dramatically, "The finest man I knew was our regimental bhisti, GUNGA DIN." Several exciting quick cuts follow: an ugly restless vulture atop a pole/a robed Indian (*Thuggee*) severing telegraph wires with a wicked-looking pick axe/a British patrol on horseback/*Thuggees* digging graves/soldiers attacked by night/fade out.

Then a longer, establishing shot takes form showing the British station at Muri, Northwest India, where the Colonel (Montagu Love) worries aloud in an English public school accent about the telegraph's ominous silence from Trantapur. In seconds, Tretheway, Jake and Wan Ho are transported back into remote late nineteenth-century British India.

● ● ●

Two significant events occurred in April, which should have triggered to Tretheway's mind the possibility of a calamitous third. The first, a break-in and burglary at the Fort York Military Museum, was certainly serious, but not high on the priority list of the FYPD, let alone Tretheway's traffic division. And the second, he didn't hear about until too late. In his defence, all divisions, especially traffic, were busy preparing for the momentous visit of King George VI and Queen Elizabeth on June 7. Parade routes had to be drawn out, new traffic patterns plotted, duties rescheduled and overall protocol studied, to say nothing of extensive security measures for their Royal British Majesties.

Tretheway had little time to worry about the theft of some old uniforms and dusty, antiquated weapons.

● ● ●

During the War of 1812, a defensive position was hastily constructed on the narrow strip of land that separated Wellington Square Bay from Coote's Paradise to repel four thousand American invaders advancing from Fort Niagara. History records that a British force of seven hundred under General John Vincent marched from this breastwork to meet the Americans halfway and turn them back at the Battle of Stoney Creek; by world standards a skirmish in a small war. But if the tables had been turned, Southern Ontario would now be called something like Very Upper New York.

Battery Lodge was built on the original breastwork. Over the years, the sturdy two-storey building housed a gatekeeper, a castle guard during the 1837 rebellion and a gardener's family until, just after WWI, it became the official Fort York Military Museum. Paintings, etchings, posters, uniforms, weapons and other historic military artifacts graced the interior of the grey building. Two bronze British nine-pounder field guns protected the entrance, then and now.

When the museum staff turned up on Wednesday morning, April 11, they found the front door ajar, with the lock broken. They called the police. When the detectives arrived, they had unkind words with Basil

Horsborough, the museum's curator, for not install-
ing an alarm system. He lisped his way through excuses from "not in the budget" to "I can't think of everything."

Basil Horsborough had been plucked from the An-
glican ministry by well-meaning relatives in high
places to head up the Military Museum. He was tall
and cadaver thin. Straight black hair, parted in the
middle and hanging over his ears, framed his pale face.
In good or troubled spirits, his unnaturally red lips
turned up at the ends. From opening to closing time,
the smiling staff watched his loose-jointed round-
shouldered rambles as he checked, re-arranged or just
fussed over his precious exhibits. He occasionally visited the Tretheways but never played cards and if he
drank anything, it was a small glass of Addie's lip-
pursing dandelion wine. Basil owned seven black suits.

The detectives (not including the off-duty Wan Ho)
went about their business searching for clues. Except
for the hundreds of fingerprints, which said little for
the museum cleaning women, they found none. And
these prints, one detective said, were probably from
tourists or staff. Several glass display cases had been
smashed or pried open. Medals, uniforms, small weapons and other personal effects of yesterday's soldiers
were strewn about the rooms, but upon inspection not
damaged. An etching of Napoleon and Blucher had
been torn, a death-of-Nelson print badly creased and
a watercolour of the Royal Field Artillery in action at
Mons slightly smudged. But what really upset Basil
were the pieces no one could find. It took him and his
staff two days to put everything back in its place and
three more to replace all the glass. The police suggested

they take careful inventory. This produced a small but thought-provoking list of missing warrior's paraphernalia.

The first item was one of the museum's prize acquisitions; a dress frock coat of an American Union Army General, 1864, reputed to have been worn by General William Tecumseh Sherman during the Civil War (a noisy political group who had opposed Horsborough's patronage appointment openly disputed its authenticity). The culprits, curiously, left a Confederate Army officer's uniform undisturbed.

A rare pilot's flying suit had disappeared along with a leather helmet, goggles and mittens that someone had once bravely worn in the unheated cockpit of a Royal Flying Corps aircraft over Flanders.

Three more uniforms or parts made the list; a WWI Royal Navy Reserve Ordinary Seaman Gunner's jacket, a Lieutenant's dress uniform (Nursing Sister) Canadian Medical Corps also from the First War and a scarlet, full dress tunic of a non-commissioned officer, 91st Regiment, Canadian Highlanders, circa 1905.

Some weapons were missing; an 1853 pattern cavalry sword with scabbard, a *Thuggee* pickaxe used against British forces in turn-of-the-century India and a 303 calibre Lee-Enfield, Mk-1 rifle, 1888, with bayonet, from the Boer War.

Two hats could not be found: a colonial pattern helmet, white with a khaki cloth covering for the field, again from the Boer War, and an officer's rakish cocked hat from the War of 1812.

A couple of truly miscellaneous items completed the list; a large French tricolour flag, singed and torn in battle (according to Horsborough, once more disputed) and a replica of British King George III's crown.

The final listings were dutifully placed in a manilla folder marked "Burglaries, April '39" and quietly filed away, so Wan Ho didn't see it. A day later the *FY Expositor* published a partial list under the colourful heading, "Missing Historic Objet De Guerre" and buried it in the back pages, so Tretheway didn't see it. Although both men were aware of the incident, a chance meeting with Basil Horsborough brought the picture into brighter focus.

● ● ●

"Hey, Basil," Jake shouted. "What are you doing here?"

Tretheway and Jake, fresh from another Safety Club radio show, stood beside their cruiser in the enclosed courtyard of Central Police Station. Eight days had passed since the Military Museum burglary.

Basil loped toward them. "It's good to see a familiar face."

"You looked troubled," Tretheway said.

"I think I'm lost," Horsborough said.

"Be careful." Jake pulled Horsborough gently out of the way as another senior officer's car entered the courtyard.

They guided the befuddled curator over to a relatively quiet corner of the yard where grass, mostly crab, grew in untidy clumps. Bushes and flowers struggled to survive in front of the worn concrete steps leading to one of the doors. The fragrance of mock orange blossoms fought with the fumes of exhaust.

"Now what's your problem?" Tretheway asked.

"Where are my things?" Horsborough said.

"What things?" Tretheway said.

"My exhibits. From the Museum break-in. Have you recovered them?"

"How would I know that?"

"We're traffic, Basil," Jake explained. "You need burglary."

"What was stolen?" Tretheway asked.

"Mostly uniforms," Horsborough said. "Irreplaceable. One was worn by General Sherman."

"But nothing to threaten the public," Tretheway said.

"There were weapons."

"Oh." Tretheway thought for a moment. "But probably old weapons."

"I'm sure they're valuable," Jake said. "But hardly dangerous."

"How about a rifle?" Horsborough said to Tretheway. "A 303 Lee-Enfield, Mark One."

"Was it in working order?" Tretheway asked. "Would it fire?"

"It had a bayonet," Horsborough persisted.

"But you wouldn't hold up a bank with it."

"What about a sword? A cavalry saber?"

"Same thing."

"The pickaxe." Horsborough wrung his bony hands excitedly. "There's a dangerous weapon."

Tretheway's patience thinned. "What the hell is a military museum doing with a pickaxe?"

"It's not an ordinary pickaxe," Horsborough said. It's a Phansigan pickaxe. From northern India. Used by a religious cult. Worshipped the Goddess Kali. They were called Thugs."

A bright distinct image flashed into Tretheway's mind of Sergeant Cutter (Cary Grant) firing his revolver at a horde of white loin-clothed enemies of the crown and brandishing a captured ugly pickaxe in his other hand. "Or *Thuggees*," he said.

"What?" Horsborough knew he had finally said something important but he didn't know what.

"Jake," Tretheway ordered, "take Basil to the burglary division."

"Right," Jake said.

"And as long as you're there, get me a copy of the report. And what was stolen." Tretheway smiled at Horsborough. "It won't hurt to read it over."

● ● ●

For the next couple of evenings, Tretheway, Jake and Wan Ho went over the list until they were bleary eyed. What Tretheway thought would clarify matters did nothing but muddy the waters.

"We're no further ahead," Tretheway said.

"Not really," Wan Ho agreed.

"I thought the list would be more helpful," Jake said. He shivered despite his heavy tweed jacket. "Shouldn't we go inside?"

Although it was balmy for late April, the time of year guaranteed a drop in the temperature at sunset. The three sleuths sat on Tretheways' back porch, not screened in yet, and watched through the budding branches of black walnuts, maples and white birches as the sun met the horizon. Forty-five degrees registered on the outdoor thermometer.

"It is getting brisk," Wan Ho agreed with Jake. He turned up the collar of his topcoat.

Tretheway pretended not to hear. He sat tranquilly with his arms folded across the colourful crest of a Fort Erie 1923 Police Games sweatshirt. His only concession to the descending mercury was a heavy woolen muffler wrapped several times around his neck.

"Let's pin this thing down." Tretheway looked at Jake. "You'd better take some notes."

"Right." Jake took his hands out of his pockets. Wan Ho handed him a notebook and pencil.

"Now once more put yourself in the Fan's head," Tretheway began. "You've seen the movies. Now you break into the Military Museum. To steal a relevant article. Which one? Or ones? Let's try something new. Work backwards. Match a stolen article to a movie we've seen in the last few weeks."

"Okay." Wan Ho spoke first. "The obvious one is the *Thuggee* pickaxe. Has to be *Gunga Din*."

"That's right," Jake said.

Tretheway nodded. "And only *Gunga Din*. Just one movie. The others are not so easy."

"Like the flying suit," Wan Ho said.

"I like *Dawn Patrol* for that one," Jake said. "Or maybe *Test Pilot*."

"Don't forget *Tailspin* or *Men With Wings*," Tretheway said.

"Or even *George Takes to the Air*." Jake smiled remembering the wild George Formby flick.

"How about the serial they showed with *The Wizard of Oz*?" Wan Ho said. "*Flying G-Men, Episode Eleven*."

"Lot of movies," Jake said.

"Get them down," Tretheway said.

Jake scribbled the information in his notebook.

"Colonial khaki helmet." Tretheway continued the list of stolen items from memory. "Boer War."

"You know," Wan Ho said. "That could be *Gunga Din* as well."

Tretheway nodded. "But my pick would be *Four Feathers*. Helluva movie."

"How about *The Little Princess*?" Jake asked.

"I didn't see that one," Tretheway said.

"Shirley Temple," Wan Ho said.

"It was about the Boer War," Jake persisted.

"Write it down." Tretheway went on. "303 Lee-Enfield rifle and bayonet. That could be from any war movie made about the late eighteen hundreds to now." He tightened his muffler against a sudden breeze. "Used one myself in 'seventeen."

"*Four Feathers* or *Gunga Din* again," Wan Ho said.

"*The Sun Never Sets*," Tretheway added.

"Even *Blockheads*," Jake chuckled.

"I liked that," Wan Ho said.

"*All Quiet on the Western Front*," Tretheway suggested.

"That's pretty old," Wan Ho said.

"But it keeps coming back." Jake defended his boss's choice.

"Let's call it a maybe," Tretheway said. He pushed ahead with the list. "Nursing Sister's uniform. Lieutenant, Canadian Medical Corps."

"*Four Girls in White*?" Jake offered.

"I'd pick *Edith Cavell*," Wan Ho said.

"Better write down *Yellow Jack*," Tretheway said.

"What about the Dr. Kildare series?" Jake asked.

"That too," Tretheway said. "The next one on the list is an ordinary seaman gunner's jacket."

"I like *Sailor of the King*," Jake said.

"So do I," Wan Ho said.

"All right," Tretheway said. "Better add *Sons of the Sea*."

"And *Our Fighting Navy*," Wan Ho said.

Jake's pencil scratched over the paper.

Tretheway pictured the list. "Scarlet full dress army tunic, 1905."

"*Four Feathers* again," Jake said.

"Or *The Drum*," Wan Ho said. "Another great movie."

"There's two more Shirley Temples," Jake said.

"How many bloody movies did she make?" Tretheway asked.

"What are they?" Wan Ho asked.

"*Wee Willie Winkie*. About the British army in India. And *Susannah of the Mounties*. Both have red coats."

"Weren't they black-and-white movies?" Wan Ho asked Jake.

"So use your imagination."

"Let's get on with it," Tretheway said. "What about the cocked hat?'

"*Kidnapped*," Wan Ho said immediately.

"*Drums Along the Mohawk*," Jake said.

"This is a pretty big field," Tretheway said. "Could be anything from *Mutiny on the Bounty* to *The Hunchback of Notre Dame*."

"Or even *Gulliver's Travels*," Jake said.

"That's a cartoon," Wan Ho said.

"Full length." Jake defended his choice. "And he wore a cocked hat."

"Include it," Tretheway said to Jake.

"What's left?" Wan Ho asked.

"The flag," Tretheway remembered. "The French tricolour."

"*Beau Geste*," Jake said. "Has to be the one."

"Why not *Suez*?" Wan Ho asked.

"Or *Algiers*. Or *Garden of Allah*," Tretheway said. "Even the old *Count of Monte Cristo*."

"They all have a French theme," Wan Ho said.

"You're right," Jake admitted. "And don't forget Stan and Ollie joined the French Foreign Legion in *Flying Deuces*."

"I don't think our Fan'll use a movie more than once," Tretheway said.

"Either do I," Wan Ho agreed.

"So let's move on," Tretheway said. "The crown. A replica crown of George III."

"In *The Adventures of Sherlock Holmes*," Wan Ho said, "the bad guys were after the British crown jewels."

"Good choice," Tretheway said.

"*The Tower of London*," Jake said. "Basil Rathbone played Richard III. That sure suggests a crown."

"So does *The Private Lives of Elizabeth and Essex*," Wan Ho said.

"There was a king in *Robin Hood*," Jake said.

"Richard the Lion-Heart," Tretheway remembered.

"What about a title with the word 'king' in it?" Wan Ho suggested.

"Eh?"

"You mean like *King of Chinatown*?" Jake asked.

"Why not?" Wan Ho said. "Or *King of Gamblers*."

"King of the Underworld."

"King of the Turf."

"I think not." Tretheway stopped their game." Don't write those down," he said to Jake.

"We must be close to the end," Wan Ho said.

"Just one left," Tretheway said. "Really two. But I've lumped them together. There's a good chance they'd be seen together in the same movie. I've left them purposely until now."

"Oh?" Jake looked at Wan Ho.

"They're special?" Wan Ho asked.

"Just a feeling." Tretheway didn't explain further. "Dress uniform frock coat, General, Union Army 1864. And an 1853 cavalry sword with scabbard."

"There was a great cavalry charge at the end of *Stagecoach*," Jake said.

"Good one," Tretheway said.

"*Dodge City* maybe," Wan Ho said. "Or *Geronimo*."

"*Union Pacific*," Jake added.

"Put them all down," Tretheway said.

"How about the daddy of all charges?" Wan Ho said. "*The Charge of the Light Brigade*."

"That would only work for the sword," Tretheway said.

"And it's old," Jake said.

"Just a couple of years," Wan Ho said.

"If you want old," Jake said, "how about *Birth of a Nation*?"

"Too old," Tretheway said. "I'd rather go the other way."

Jake and Wan Ho looked puzzled.

Tretheway explained. "I talked to Freeman Thake. He told me they get advance notice of coming attractions with a synopsis that he or his employees could read, if they're interested. Only a couple of days ahead. Unless there's a special event."

Jake and Wan Ho still looked puzzled.

"There's a biggy coming up for the West End. Late July," Tretheway went on. "I've heard about it. And I'm sure you have. Lots of publicity. Even in Fort York. And the American Civil War plays a big part."

"Oh." Wan Ho came to life. "The Margaret Mitchell book."

Jake snapped his fingers. *"Gone With the Wind."*

"Right," Tretheway said. "A natural for the uniform and sword."

"And General Sherman?" Wan Ho asked.

Tretheway shrugged.

Jake wrote down *Gone With the Wind*.

"How many does that give us?" Tretheway asked.

Jake flipped through the pages of his notebook. "I make it just over forty movies."

"That many?" Wan Ho asked.

"And that's not counting the ones we haven't seen yet," Jake said.

"Plus twelve stolen items," Tretheway summed up.

"Surely the Fan isn't planning on using them all?" Jake asked.

"Just one or two, I'd say. But he probably took others in hopes of finding a relevant movie," Tretheway surmised. "And a couple more just to throw us off the track."

"Like which ones?" Jake asked.

"Maybe the cocked hat," Wan Ho suggested.

"Maybe." Tretheway shook his head. "But don't

forget what he did with the bowler." He shifted in the jumbo wicker armchair, jamming his hands as far as they would go into his warm armpits.

After a few minutes of thoughtful, discouraging silence, Wan Ho spoke.

"I take it there's nothing we can do right now?"

"Just enjoy the evening."

The temperature had dropped with the sun. An owl hooted frigidly in the darkness. The intermittent night breeze steadied.

"Invigorating," Tretheway said. His breath hung, a frosty veil, in front of his face.

"Albert." Addie opened the back door. "Come on in. You'll catch your death out there. I've made some hot chocolate."

Jake and Wan Ho lost no time in accepting Addie's invitation. Tretheway followed, grumbling.

Chapter

7

The second significant event happened a few days later, April 26, a Wednesday. But Tretheway didn't hear about it until Friday.

Addie slid the doors of the parlour open. "It's for you, Albert." She was up later than usual preparing food for a boarder's Saturday graduation party. "It's Charles Wan Ho," she announced before retiring to the kitchen.

Jake looked up from his Hornblower novel. "It's late for him," he said to Tretheway.

Tretheway pushed himself out of the soft chair. Cigar ashes flew. Wayne King music oozed from the radio. "What's the time?" he asked.

"About twenty after eleven," Jake said.

"He must be working." Tretheway went to the hall phone. Jake followed.

"This may or may not be important." Wan Ho's voice crackled through the phone with no preamble.

"Go ahead." Tretheway bent over and held the receiver upright between his own and Jake's ears.

"Speak up. Jake's listening."

"I'm at Central. A report just crossed my desk. A large, freshly dug hole was discovered by a Mr and Mrs Coombes in their backyard. Southwest area. 175 Chedoke Avenue. The street runs north and south to the Fort York mountain. It backs onto a creek, then the Fort York municipal golf course. Also called Chedoke."

Jake nodded. "I know the course," he whispered to Tretheway.

"The report's dated Thursday morning. Yesterday," Wan Ho continued. "That means the hole was dug sometime Wednesday night."

"You called me close to midnight to tell me about a hole in someone's backyard?" Tretheway questioned.

"There's more," Wan Ho said. "I talked to the investigating officer. He said it was an oblong hole about seven by four feet. And six feet deep. Very neat. The earth piled tidily close by. Sod stacked carefully to one side. He said it looked like a grave."

"Oh?" Tretheway's interest rose.

"Remember the movie *Gunga Din*?" Wan Ho said.

"Very well," Tretheway answered. Jake felt a slight shiver travel across his back.

"Didn't the *Thugees* dig graves for their victims?" Wan Ho asked.

"They did," Jake said. "Ahead of time."

"Even so," Tretheway argued, "it's still just a hole in the ground. Unless you have any other . . ."

"I do," Wan Ho interrupted. "At the end of the movie, Gunga Din warned the whole damned British

army, saving them from certain annihilation, by playing a bugle. It so happens that Mr Coombes, or really
Bugle-Major Coombes, is the leader of the Royal FY
Light Infantry Bugle Band. He's probably the city's best
known bugler." Wan Ho paused to let his information
sink in. "Would you like to call on the Coombses tomorrow?"

"No," Tretheway said.

Jake looked surprised.

"But . . ." Wan Ho started.

"Tonight," Tretheway said.

"Eh?"

"We'll meet you there," Tretheway ordered.

● ● ●

Sometime during Tretheway's late night, three-way
phone conversation, Bugle-Major Reginald F. Coombes's studded military boots clicked down the metal
steps of the FY Street Railway car stopped at the bottom of his street.

As anyone who took the trouble to find out knew,
the RFYLI Bugle Band (Reserve) practised every Tuesday and paraded with the regiment every Friday. Both
evenings ended convivially. The band's Mess came
alive with WWI reminiscences, bawdy military songs
and Niagara-On-The-Lake Camp legends mellowed
by past tellings, all washed down with countless jugs
of nut brown ale.

Acknowledging the friendly clanging bell of the
departing streetcar with a casual salute, Bugle-Major
Coombes marched smartly, if unsteadily, up Chedoke
Avenue toward his home. Despite a wind-whipped
misty drizzle, a tight little smile appeared on his

weatherbeaten face as he swaggered rhythymically in front of his imaginary band. Long ago pictures of his wartime service, enhanced by memory and alcohol, materialized before his eyes as the shrill, exciting sounds of the band filled his head. Bugles blared "The Old Contemptibles" in pure, bitten-off notes. Drumsticks crashed smartly on thinly stretched drumheads in perfect staccato accompaniment.

As he raised a make-believe baton and right-wheeled into his gravel driveway, a dark turbaned figure, swathed in loincloth, left the cover of a spirea bush and, from behind, looped a thin deadly garrote around his neck. The last words Bugle-Major Coombes heard were, "Kill for the love of Kali."

●　●　●

"Won't this thing go any faster?" Tretheway said.

"It's not warmed up yet," Jake answered.

Tretheway twisted in his seat as much as he could toward Jake. "It didn't start up too well either."

"It's wet," Jake alibied. "Starts beautifully if you give it a chance."

Tretheway grunted.

The wipers swept hypnotically across the windshield as the '33 Pontiac's cold engine protested Jake's rough handling. He pushed the heavy vehicle over the glistening roads at speeds on the edge of safety. When they turned up the incline of Chedoke Avenue, another car fell in behind them. A flash of headlights reflected from the Pontiac's rear-view mirror .

"Must be Wan Ho," Jake said.

Tretheway grunted again.

Jake parked his customary foot-and-a-half from the curb in front of number 175. Wan Ho pulled in behind. The front verandah light shone through the mist. Other lights lit up the ground floor of the house.

"Looks like they're still up," Jake said. He joined Wan Ho on the sidewalk.

They waited while Tretheway planted both feet in the space between the car and the curb and pulled himself out of the sunken leather passenger seat.

"Should we go around to the back?" Wan Ho asked.

"Better go to the front door," Tretheway said. "Don't want to alarm the Coombeses."

Jake looked around at the other, mostly darkened, homes. "Or the neighbours," he said.

The three padded up the wet flagstone walk. Tretheway reached for the door. His outstretched arm was inches from the Coombes's ornate, solid brass doorknocker, a replica of an RFYLI hat badge, when an unbelievably loud crash of breaking glass reverberated around the house.

"What the hell?"

"Where'd that come from?" Jake asked.

"Don't know," Wan Ho said.

A high, piercing, hair-raising scream followed a split second later.

"That's from inside." Tretheway banged the doorknocker. "Police!"

Another scream erupted.

Tretheway tried the door. It didn't open. "Damn!" His 275 pounds lunged at the thick oaken barrier. The Yale lock tore from the inside frame as the door banged open. A third scream, just as loud as the first two, pinpointed the source. Tretheway led the charge across the elegant foyer, past the curving staircase and through the kitchen to burst awkwardly into a sunken family room that stretched across the rear of the house. Mrs Coombes stood, hands on cheeks, in front of a shattered picture window. Shards of glass littered the floor. In the centre of a deep, hand-carved oriental carpet, highlighted eerily by a chandelier now swinging in the wind from the open window, lay the object hurled through the glass minutes before; a *Thuggee* pickaxe.

"Police," Tretheway said again. He fumbled for his badge, then realized it was in his uniform at home.

"Jake," he said.

Jake pushed his hands into his own pockets. He shook his head.

Mrs Coombes prepared for a fourth scream.

Wan Ho quickly held out his badge. "Sergeant Wan Ho, Ma'am." He pointed to Tretheway and Jake. "Inspector Tretheway and Constable Small. FYPD."

"They don't look like policemen," Mrs Coombes said.

"I'm sorry, Mrs Coombes," Tretheway said. "But this is an emergency." He pointed to the pickaxe. "I assume that was thrown through the window?"

Mrs Coombes frowned suspiciously but nodded.

"Did you see who threw it?" Tretheway asked.

"Yes I did," Mrs Coombes said, recovering. "An Indian."

"Pardon?"

"An East Indian. Right out of Rudyard Kipling. Wearing a white sheet and a, you know," she swirled a finger around her head, "a turban. Like Sabu."

"You're sure?" Tretheway questioned.

"Yes. He just stood there. Beside the hole in the ground." She paused for a moment. "Almost as if he wanted me to see him."

"Sergeant," Tretheway ordered. "You stay with Mrs Coombes."

"But . . ." Wan Ho began.

"Let's go," Tretheway said to Jake. He started for the side door. Jake followed looking back helplessly at Wan Ho.

"Be careful of the creek," Mrs Coombes shouted after them."

Outside the wet darkness closed around them.

"The flashlight's in the car," Jake said.

"No time." Tretheway jogged through the back-yard, skirting the barely discernible hole with the neat pile and sod still beside it, to the edge of the hallow gorge now in deep shadow.

Jake caught up. "There's the golf course." He pointed across the gorge to where what light there was showed a relatively flat, but rolling, cultivated land-scape. No figures could be seen.

"He must be down there somewhere." Tretheway started rashly down the steep, uneven incline through misshapen rocks and long wild grass. Jake took a more lateral, safer descent.

"Damn." Tretheway's curse was easily heard over the gurgling spring run-off.

"What's the matter?" Jake shouted.

"Nothing." Tretheway tried to remember the last time he got a soaker.

"There's some flat stones down here," Jake shouted. "I think we can get over the creek."

"Forget it," Tretheway shouted.

"What?" Jake scrambled back. Tretheway leaned against a tree pouring creek water from his boot onto the ground.

"He's gone," Tretheway said quietly. "He's made his point. Left the *Thuggee* axe. Made sure Mrs Coombes saw him."

"You mean he got away?" Jake asked.

Tretheway nodded. "I just wonder."

"Hm?"

"Where do you suppose Mr Coombes is?"

"The Bugle-Major?"

Tretheway nodded. "It didn't look like he was in the house."

Jake's neck went prickly. "No, it didn't."

"And why do you suppose our Indian friend was standing beside the alleged grave?"

Jake didn't answer.

"We'd better have a look."

"You're not thinking . . ."

"Now we need the flashlight," Tretheway interrupted.

Jake ran to the car. By the time he got back to the grave, Tretheway was already there, bent over, hands leaning on his muscular thighs, staring into the dark hole. The swirling mist verged on rain.

"There's something there," Tretheway said.

Jake switched on the flashlight. Bugle-Major Coombes lay on his back, arms neatly folded over his midsection. The beam of light picked out the brilliant scarlet and gold of the Bugler's braid across his chest. Large drops of moisture from the trees splashed onto his face, washing away some of the token clay clods thrown onto the grave. The small tight smile remained.

"Gawd." Jake switched the light off.

● ● ●

Two cruisers, an unmarked car with detectives, a *FY Expo* reporter with photographer and Doc Nooner, all appeared shortly after Tretheway's call to Central. Chief Constable Horace Zulp arrived last. His sirens awoke the residents who had managed to sleep through the first part of the investigation.

"Strangled," Doc Nooner said to Zulp. "Some sort of garrote. Wire, rope, cloth."

Tretheway and Wan Ho stood in the warm dryness of the Coombes's family room within earshot of Zulp. Jake positioned himself behind them. Relevant activity hummed in the background. One neighbour made coffee. Another comforted Mrs Coombes in the adjacent living room. Detectives bustled. Mud spots showed on everyone's clothing, evidence of graveside examinations, especially Doc Nooner's.

"And not too long ago," the doctor concluded.

"I'd say around midnight."

Zulp stared at Tretheway. "Isn't that when you got here?" His deep, imperious voice took over the room.

"Yes sir," Tretheway answered.

Chief Zulp lapsed into one of his meaningful not-to-be-interrupted silences. He bobbed up and down on the balls of his feet, hands clasped behind him. His lower lip pushed in and out thoughtfully. When in doubt, Zulp went by the book. But when flushed with confidence, he went by intuition, usually wrong. He spoke in short, ungrammatical phrases.

"Did you see him?" Zulp asked.

"Sir?"

"The murderer. Perpetrator." Zulp shook his heavy jowls impatiently. "The Indian."

"No, sir," Tretheway answered. "Just missed him."

"But you gave pursuit?"

"Yes, sir."

Zulp pulled at his bulbous nose. "Why?"

Tretheway looked puzzled. "To try and catch him."

"No. No." Zulp's jowls shook again. "Why are you here?"

Tretheway was always caught off guard by the Chief's unpredictable, rabbit-like, train-of-thought jumps.

"Was there a traffic problem?" Zulp pressed.

"No, sir."

"Well?"

"It was a movie."

"Eh?"

"*Gunga Din.*"

Another meaningful silence followed. Zulp's forehead creased as he checked the room. Activity still buzzed around them. Doc Nooner excused himself silently to accompany the Bugle-Major downtown. A flashbulb popped outside. Zulp noticed that no one else in his immediate group looked confused. He lowered his voice. "Perhaps you should explain."

For the next few moments Tretheway, with the help of Jake and Wan Ho, filled in the chief as best he could. He started with *Gunga Din*, then rationalized his conclusions with *Flying Deuces* and touched on the combination of *Only Angels Have Wings* and the Dundurn aviary vandalism. The Military Museum burglary came briefly into the discussion. At the end of his explanation, Tretheway sensed that Zulp's eyes had glazed over about halfway through. He waited. Eventually Zulp spoke.

"You're telling me that the killer of Bugle-Major Coombes was inspired by a movie?"

Tretheway nodded.

"*Gunga Din*?" Zulp said.

Tretheway nodded again.

"And it happened before. Twice. With Laurel and Hardy. And the escaped bird."

"Condor," Tretheway corrected.

"Do you know why someone is doing this?"

Tretheway had to shake his head.

"Horse with a hat. Stolen bird. Bhisti bugler. All with no motive." Zulp's lower lip went into action again. "You know what I think? You live in the movies. Fantasy land. Celluloid city. Tretheway, you've got to get down to earth. Reality." His eyes bulged. "Steelmaking. Garbage. '39 Plymouths. Traffic jams. That's reality."

"But what about the grave?" Tretheway argued. "And the pickaxe? The garroting? A lot of coincidence there."

"That's the first thing you've said that holds water."

"Sir?"

"Coincidence." Zulp started bobbing again. "As simple as that."

"But . . ."

"Did it ever cross your mind that the killer really is from India? What did you call him? A *Thuggee*? That the Bugle-Major was involved in some cult? Mystery of the East?" He unclasped his hands long enough to wag a finger at Tretheway. "Use your imagination. But keep both feet on the ground. Don't be swayed by some Rudyard Kipling fairy tale."

Tretheway's large abdomen heaved quietly.

"So starting tomorrow," Zulp continued, "a proper investigation. Leadership. Sanity returns. Back to the real world." He glared at Tretheway. "You. Back to traffic." His eyes flitted to Jake and came to rest on Wan Ho. "And first thing in the morning, Sergeant, round up all the Indians."

Chapter

8

For the next week Tretheway and Jake sat by and watched as Zulp directed his whirlwind investigation. One of the unearthed facts showed that Bugle-Major Coombes had indeed served in India for about six months during WWI, albeit in the wrong theatre for *Thuggee* activity. Zulp still took this as confirmation of his theory. The detectives, including Wan Ho, did dutifully round up all the East Indians in Fort York. There were seven. They ranged from an FYU professor of Eastern Philosophy and History to an incompetent fakir abandoned by a travelling carnival. By Friday it had been proven conclusively that, because of age, religion, caste, district or availability, not one of them came close to the target. Undaunted, Zulp merely assumed the perpetrator had escaped. He saw that descriptive bulletins were sent out to brother police departments in Southern Ontario, Quebec, the Maritimes and several neighbouring states in the U.S. "Now we'll see what the net brings in," he was overheard to say.

As ordered, Tretheway went back to the traffic business. He and Jake also went back to the movies.

The month of May was no slacker in the variety of entertaining films. *Young Mr. Lincoln, Prison Farm, Out West With the Hardys, Confessions of a Nazi Spy, Topper Takes a Trip, Orphans of the Street* ("alone in the world with his dog") and *Treasure Island* flickered across the West End's silver screen. Tretheway passed on *Women Against Women, Annabella* ("it's the season for romance"), *Three Loves for Nancy* and *Bridal Suite* on the strength of their titles. Wan Ho joined them for *The Saint Strikes Back, The Lady Vanishes* and *Bulldog Drummond's Secret Police*. Addie chose to view Bette Davis in *Dark Victory* and *Three Smart Girls Grow Up*. Miles Terminus and Doc Nooner at different times took in about half a dozen films, Bartholemew Gum saw close to half while Jake, as usual, didn't miss a flick.

Early in the month, a Tuesday, Tretheway and Jake, accompanied this time by Gum and Terminus, entered the world of desert warfare, brotherly devotion, white sapphires, beautiful gestures, Viking funerals and the French Foreign Legion. They saw *Beau Geste.* In a powerful opening scene, a relief column of Legionnaires marching across the Sahara halt a short distance from a strangely quiet Fort Linderneuf. An officer with a trumpeter leaves his troops to investigate. They circle the fort and find at each crenellation a lifeless Legionnaire staring glassily back at them, his long rifle pointing rigidly toward the sandswept horizon. The trumpeter scales the wall and drops inside. He never returns. The mystery deepens.

● ● ●

On Wednesday, the last day of May, the clement weather continued into the night. Fleecy clouds vainly chased the bright moon. Stars glittered. Moonlight reflected brokenly on the rippley waters of Fort York Harbour. The clear conditions made it easy for the three man crew of the *Judge Millander* to spot the fireboat. The same breeze that pushed the clouds across the sky easily carried the crackling of flames over the open water.

"What the hell's that?" the Skipper shouted. He spun the wheel of the small tug-cum-police-boat toward the burning vessel.

"A boat on fire," the second crew member answered.

"Looks like a sailboat," the third said.

As they closed in, the dry cotton sail of the flaming boat exploded in a fireball that for an instant lit up the whole of Fort York Harbour. But it seemed to expend the fire's strength. By the time the *Judge Millander*'s steel hull nudged the wooden sailboat, the fire appeared manageable. Buckets of sand and water from the tug, along with more water from a primitive but effective stirrup pump, turned the remaining flames into heavy smoke.

With the two boats roughly grappled together, the Skipper ran the beam of the tug's high-powered spotlight up and down the length of the smouldering craft. Crewman number three jumped aboard. He prodded a turning bulge with a boat hook.

"Gawd."

"What is it?" the Skipper shouted.

"Looks like a body."

"What?"

"With his arms crossed. Like he was laid out."

The Skipper swung the spotlight to where the crewman pointed. A partially scorched cadaver stood out starkly in the harsh light. The crewman stumbled backward over another, smaller lump at its feet.

"Gawd," he said again.

"Now what?"

"I think it's a dog."

The beam of light swung away.

"Don't touch anything," the Skipper ordered. "Rig up a tow and come aboard. Quickly." He picked up the ship-to-shore that connected the police boat to Central.

The *Judge Millander* chugged shoreward, its smoking funeral pyre in tow.

● ● ●

June first fell on a Thursday. Chief Zulp's head throbbed. His skin appeared more leathery, more creased and, despite a nine o'clock bath, he looked unkempt. Strands of unruly grey hair stood on end and pointed in different directions. A smudge marred his celluloid collar. He had been awake most of the night heading up the murder investigation.

"Well, Tretheway?" Zulp's deep tone approached plaintive. His net had brought in nothing. Never backward about jumping on the appropriate bandwagon, he had called Tretheway in to pursue the movie theory. "What do you make of it?"

Tretheway adjusted his bulk in the confining wooden armchair. He and Basil Horsborough were both fresh from a good night's sleep. Horsborough had been called downtown to identify the remnants of the stolen French tricolour and the charred but salvageable Mark One Lee-Enfield rifle with bayonet, both found on the burned sailboat. They sat directly in front of Zulp's formidable desk. A heavy-lidded Wan Ho shared the slippery leather sofa with a bright-eyed Jake. Zulp and Wan Ho had briefed everyone on the night's events. It was now mid-morning.

Tretheway looked at Jake. "I don't think there's any doubt."

Jake nodded. "There's only one movie that fits."

"*Beau Geste*," Tretheway said.

"Bo what?" Zulp said.

"Geste," Tretheway said. "A family name. There were three brothers. Beau, a nickname for Michael, Digby and John. They ran away from England, a question of family honour, to join the Foreign Legion. A beau geste. Or beautiful gesture. Double entendre."

"You see," Jake began, "one of them stole a rare sapphire from Lady Brandon . . ."

"What has all this got to do with a burning boat in the middle of Fort York Harbour?" Zulp interrupted.

"We're coming to it," Tretheway said. He decided to skip over the opening sequence of dead defenders.

"There's a flashback that shows the Geste brothers as children. They give Beau a pretend Viking's funeral. A toy sailboat. A tin soldier stands in for Beau. A tiny Union Jack to cover him up. Toy weapons. And also in keeping with Viking tradition, a pet. In this case a china dog. They set the whole thing on fire and push the boat out into the pond. Beau makes them promise to give him the same send-off when he grows up. When he really dies. Kids would promise something like that." Tretheway looked around. He noticed that although Zulp showed a slight impatience, so far his eyes had not turned to glass. "So, near the end of the movie," he continued, "after Beau is killed at Fort Zinderneuf, his brothers once again give him a Viking's funeral. Of course there's no boat. They put him in his bunk. With his weapons. Cover him with the French flag, the only one available, and start the fire."

"Don't forget the dog," Jake said.

Tretheway smiled. "That was a nice touch. No dog. So they laid Sergeant Markoff at his feet."

"Sergeant Markoff was the villain," Jake explained.

"Is that relevant?" Zulp asked.

"Not really," Jake said.

"Then get on with it." Zulp rubbed his temples.

"Our Fan tried to duplicate the movie," Tretheway said. "As best he could. The burning boat, I'm sure stolen. The dog, probably a stray. The rifle and flag from the museum." He looked at Wan Ho. "And you say the murdered man was a vagrant."

"That's right," Wan Ho said. "Looks like an arbitrary choice. Target of opportunity."

"Maybe," Tretheway said. "But he was a tramp. A knight of the open road."

"What are you getting at?" Wan Ho asked.

"A hobo," Tretheway said. "Sometimes shortened to Bo."

Wan Ho whistled.

"I never thought of that," Jake said. "How was he killed?"

"Doc Nooner's still working on it," Wan Ho said.

"It doesn't matter," Tretheway said. "Our Fan simply needed a body."

After a short silence, Zulp spoke. "Is that it?"

"Except for the sailboat," Tretheway said.

"Eh?"

"The central theme of *Beau Geste* was a stolen gem. All events revolved around a sapphire. It gave meaning to the title."

"So?" Zulp said.

"It was called the Blue Water."

"The name of the sailboat," Wan Ho said.

Tretheway nodded. So did Jake.

"So the boat wasn't a random choice?" Wan Ho asked.

"No," Tretheway said. "It was calculated. We're dealing with a planner."

Everyone sat with his thoughts for a moment.

Horsborough broke the quiet. "When can I have my rifle and bayonet back?"

Zulp ignored him. "I have to admit it's a strong case. Plausible," he admitted. "But where are we going? Still no motive." He looked at Tretheway. "What now?"

Tretheway shrugged. "It's hard to predict."

Jake and Wan Ho shook their heads.

Zulp leaned back in his high, throne-like chair. He stared at the ceiling. Everyone ogled the quivering folds of his neck as he did his lip thing. *"Birth of a Nation,"* he said.

"Pardon?" Tretheway said.

"Last movie I saw. Couldn't get into it. No sound. No colour." Zulp dropped his gaze. He stood up abruptly, shooting his wheeled chair into the wall behind. "Back to business," he said, signalling the end of the meeting.

That evening Zulp attended his first movie in over twenty years.

● ● ●

Back to business for Wan Ho and the detectives meant running down the few precious leads of the previous night. They traced the owner of the *Blue Water* easily enough, but he hadn't used the boat for a week. It had been moored across the bay with a fleet of small boats loosely connected under the name, Wellington Square Yacht Club; no dues, no clubhouse, only seven moorings, and at that time of night, deserted.

The victim was officially declared a John Doe, killed by a blow to the head before the burning, and the dog a stray. A positive note was the recovery of one Lee-Enfield rifle with bayonet. Basil Horsborough accepted the weapon gratefully but did little to hide his disappointment about the irreplaceable French tricolour.

Leads fizzled. The investigation bogged down until it was expediently pushed aside for other matters. The seemingly senseless killing of a vagrant and a stray dog paled beside the imminent, once-in-a-lifetime Royal Visit.

Which is what back to business meant to Tretheway. He and Jake spent all their time up to the 2:45 Wednesday afternoon arrival of the Sovereigns checking and re-checking the parade route, traffic control, barricades, dress codes, protocol and the logistics of moving men and vehicles during the procession. These worrisome details kept them busy and away from other activities, even the movies.

Although the King's and Queen's stay was to end at 4:09 the same afternoon, it was the longest and most carefully organized hour and a half in the history of Fort York. Except for a skeleton staff manning the police stations, all one hundred and sixty of FY's finest drew street duty. As well, eighty-five Toronto policemen (including ten motorcyclists), fifty FY firemen sworn in as Special Constables, an RCMP Detachment and CN Railway Police fleshed out the FYPD ranks to control the expected three hundred thousand spectators.

On the auspicious day, even the weather fell into line. As though by proclamation a royal golden sun shone in a royal blue sky. This did little however to soothe Tretheway's impatience as he awaited the Royal Couple. He headed up a group of ten FY policemen, twenty more from Toronto and ten RCMP Redcoats, all fidgety, at the CN station. When the King and Queen stepped down from the train on time, organized chaos broke loose. The RFYLI Brass Band struck up "God Save The King." An army officer unfurled the Royal Standard. The RFYLI honour guard presented arms. All senior police officers saluted. Puffs of smoke blossomed on the mountain brow as a twenty-one-gun salute rumbled from the 11th Battery, Royal Canadian

Artillery. Cheers rose from the reserved bleachers.

On the dias, Prime Minister Mackenzie King took minutes to present the reception party. Tretheway, not a member of the official party, still managed to edge close enough to the Royal Pair just in case. He scanned the crowd while saluting. Surely, he thought, even someone as bold as the Fan wouldn't dare. . . .

Spontaneous cheers from citizens lining the route engulfed the motorcade as it headed south on James Street. Chief Zulp rode in the first car with, and in awe of, the Chief Constable of Scotland Yard Metropolitan Police. The King and Queen smiled incessantly and waved to their subjects from an open, four-door maroon convertible driven by a Mountie and flying another Royal Standard. Four more cars carrying local diginitaries and members of the Royal party followed. Doc Nooner travelled in the sixth car with the Royal physician and an equerry-in-waiting.

A similar reception took place at the city hall with more salutes, more militia and another honour guard. But this time the Mayor and City Council met the Royal Pair. And the Argyll and Sutherland Highlanders' Brass Band played the national anthem. The crowd sang. Everyone cheered.

The parade continued south from city hall. Every possible vantage point held someone waving, shaking a flag, cheering or at least smiling. Children straddled the bronze lions at the foot of Queen Victoria's statue for a better view. Others hung from trees. Everywhere red, white and blue bunting decorated the buildings. Bands stationed every quarter mile filled the air with martial music. Veterans, militia, auxiliary police and St. John's Ambulance members bordered the parade route in front of the applauding spectators, some into their fourth hour of waiting. Plainclothesmen, including Wan Ho, infiltrated the crowds looking for pickpockets or potentially embarrassing characters (Crazy Mary or Drop-pants Harvey to mention two) to forestall any humiliating incidents. Wan Ho shared Tretheway's anxious thoughts about the Fan as his eyes skipped from face to face.

At the same time that the procession turned east on Main Street to begin its longest leg, the police detachment at city hall jumped into pre-arranged cars and buses and roared along back streets leapfrogging to the next stop, Scott Park. Minutes before that, Tretheway's group had boarded a pilot train and chugged through Fort York's north end on their way to Jockey Club Siding, the point of Royal departure.

When the cavalcade turned north onto Melrose Avenue toward Scott Park, it soon passed the home of Freeman Thake. The West End owner had graciously and democratically offered his spacious front verandah to his staff for an enviable view of the Royal Couple. He had also invited a few friends, among them Addie, Miles Terminus and Basil Horsborough. Addie waved at the motorcade every bit as graciously as the Queen. Terminus stood stiffly at attention while Horsborough, smiling quietly, arms fully extended, held a large, red and white cross-of-St.George flag he had borrowed from the museum, in front of his black suit. Neil Heavenly and Joshua Pike shook miniature Union Jacks. Lulu Ashcroft jumped up and down excitedly waving both arms and bouncing both breasts.

Violet Farrago shouted wildly. And Thake beamed continuously as though he had arranged the whole spectacle for another added attraction. Addie said afterward that the Queen looked right at her but then, everyone on the verandah said the same thing.

When the procession turned into Scott Park, the second loudest cheer of the day escaped the throats of thirty thousand waiting school children. Somewhere in the throng, Scouter Gum and his troop added to the din. Girl Guides and Brownies squealed. Bemedalled men wearing white ducks, blue blazers and dashing straw boaters led platoons of flag-bearing athletes around the quarter-mile cinder track past the reviewing stand. The King saluted, the Queen waved. Twelve hundred white-clad school children overflowed the infield and performed a well-rehearsed show of calisthenics. After a Royal aside ("Aren't the children splendid?") the King proclaimed the next day a school holiday, thus eliciting the loudest cheer of the day.

By the time the cortege had left Scott Park, Tretheway and his men had already reinforced the contingent at the Jockey Club. Once again the process was repeated with a different cast; another presentation, more curtsies, cheering, handshakes and waving, an honour guard of thirty-two Rover Scouts and a final twenty-one-gun salute. The Royal Couple, unbelievably still smiling and waving, watched from the observation platform of the departing train as the colourful vista of Fort York receded. In a parting fillip, a group of urchins outflanked the Canadian National Railway Police and chased down the track after the puffing train waving flags and pennants until their breath ran out. The King and Queen were amused.

At that moment the city also ran out of breath, or so it seemed to Tretheway. Fort York began a short period of post-Royal Visit depression. Months of preparations had climaxed in a whirlwind hour and a half. And now everybody had to go back to ordinary life, back to routine, Tretheway included.

Parties were held that night to celebrate a job well done. But mostly, people turned in early. Except for school children and teachers, tomorrow was another workday. Tretheway spent the evening at home rehashing the events of the momentous day and comparing notes with drop-in friends. No one stayed late. Miles Terminus, Horsborough and Gum had left about ten. Addie went to bed shortly after that. Tretheway and Jake sat at the kitchen table sharing a beer. They had just closed the door behind Wan Ho. Addie's small radio played the music of Ted Weems. Tretheway thumbed through the special souvenir Royal Visit Edition of the *FY Expo* searching for news. Wedged between dozens of ads all headed "Welcome To Their Majesties," he found a few headlines.

"Chamberlain Says Hitler Will Not Bring On War," Tretheway read aloud. "Military Experts Confident Polish Cavalry Can Contain German Army. Berlin Practices Air Raid Drills." He shook his head. "Very discouraging news." He picked up another section and was halfway through a comic strip ad story of how, if one used Lifebuoy Soap to stop B.O., one could gain rapid promotion and enter a happy marriage, when Jake spoke.

"When all is considered then, the day went well?"

"Better than I expected." Tretheway put the paper down.

"You expected something?"

"Not really." Tretheway took a long pull of Molson Blue. His eyes widened as his upper body convulsed in a quiet belch. "But every time I looked at the crowd, I half expected our friend to do something silly."

"I must say it crossed my mind," Jake admitted.

"But I guess he hadn't seen the right movie," Tretheway said.

"You really think that's why he didn't do anything?"

"Among other things."

"Like?"

"Security. You must admit it was tight."

Jake nodded.

"And it was too close to the last one," Tretheway explained. "He seems to need a gestation period. A few weeks at least to choose a suitable movie. Prepare the events. Make necessary arrangements." He drained his quart. "And then there's the most logical reason."

"Which is?"

Tretheway put his empty on the kitchen table. "He wanted to see the King and Queen."

"You're joking."

"Not at all. He was probably waving a bloody flag. And cheering."

"A fine King's subject."

"A patriot."

"So what do we do now?" Jake asked.

"Just what he's going to do."

"Eh?"

"Go to the movies."

Jake smiled. "Why not?"

"Maybe tomorrow." Tretheway smiled back.

"Right." Jake stood up. "I'm for the sack."

Tretheway pointed to the ice box. "As long as you're up."

Jake handed his boss a frosted bottle of ale.

Chapter

9

Tretheway and Jake did return to the movies, the next night.

In honour of the Royal Visit, Freeman Thake had used his influence to procure the most kingly or queenly movies he could for that week. He ran the pair an unprecedented six consecutive days. So on Thursday Tretheway and Jake sat through *The Private Lives of Elizabeth and Essex*, a vivid technicolour costume drama of royal court intrigue, more fiction than history. It revolved around the love/hate relationship of Elizabeth I of England (Bette Davis) and the Earl of Essex (Errol Flynn) in their struggle for power. Essex eventually lost his head.

The second feature stuck closer to fact. A gory historical thriller, *The Tower of London*, follows the deformed, evil Richard III (Basil Rathbone) as he kills and tortures his way to the fifteenth-century English throne. Boris Karloff plays Mord, a club-footed, handy-with-the-axe executioner. The Duke of Clarence (Vincent Price) gives a satisfying, blood-curdling performance when he drowns horribly in a vat of Malmsey wine. *The Tower of London* appealed to Tretheway while Jake, a fan of Errol Flynn's since *Captain Blood*, preferred the first feature.

For the rest of June and into the first week of July, Tretheway and Jake, with assorted happenstance companions, viewed a varied slate of feature attractions. And with certain exceptions, they agreed any one of them could goad an unbalanced killer into another murderous scheme. Movies like *Last Warning, Street of Missing Men, Boy Slaves* ("seething story of wayward youth"), *Trapped in the Sky, Crime Takes a Holiday* or even *The Gracie Allen Murder Case* were all possible fodder for the creative but warped mind of the Fan. Addie accompanied Jake for the ostensibly harmless exceptions; *Romance of the Limberlost, Zenobia* and *Good Girls Go to Paris*. Tretheway skipped all of these as well as *Ice Follies of '39*.

● ● ●

"Sorry to bother you this late on a Sunday," Wan Ho said.

"That's okay," Jake answered. "We're still up."

"I'm calling from Central."

"Pull night duty again?"

"Zulp loves me."

Tretheway came out of the parlour. "Who's that?"

"Wan Ho."

Then Jake spoke into the mouthpiece. "We're both here."

"Just got a call." Wan Ho raised his voice so both Tretheway and Jake could hear. Jake held the receiver between them. "A Mrs D.W. Clarence, 53 Mayfair. That's not far from you. Reported a prowler."

"I take it not your usual prowler," Tretheway

"You tell me," Wan Ho said. "She heard a noise in the backyard. Thought it was D.W., that's her husband, returning from walking the dogs. Switched on the back porch lights. Saw a man. She thinks a man. Close to the window. Wild unruly hair. Laughing. Jumping up and down. Drinking from a bottle. He appeared deformed. Crookback was her word." He paused. "You still with me?"

"Go on," Tretheway said.

"She screamed," Wan Ho went on. "Now get this. He took another drink from the bottle. Then carefully put it down on the back porch. In no hurry. Sound familiar?"

"As though he wanted to be seen," Tretheway said.

"Exactly," Wan Ho said. "One more thing. He was wearing a crown."

"A crown. A King's crown."

"Definitely not your usual prowler," Jake said.

"Sound nutsy enough to be our Movie Fan?" Wan Ho asked.

Tretheway and Jake exchanged nods.

"Did you see *The Tower of London*?" Tretheway spoke into the mouthpiece.

"No," Wan Ho said.

"You'd better pick us up on your way," Tretheway ordered. He took the receiver from Jake's hand and hung up.

● ● ●

Mayfair Crescent ran by the sprawling FY University campus, past its playing fields, sunken gardens and ivy-covered seats of learning, before it looped back on itself. Except for a few residents, the secluded loop was used in the daytime by young persons learning to drive and when night fell by more young persons, still in cars, learning the rituals of love making. "Sort of a vehicular Flirtation Walk," Addie would say. In the enclosed elongated oval, several magnificent oaks stood above smaller scrub trees. At their foot, Queen Ann's lace, shimmering blue cornflowers, goldenrod and wild grasses grew tall between monthly cuttings by the FY Parks Department. On the side across from the University property were three houses. Each occupied a landscaped acre. The Clarences lived in the first one.

Old Cyrus Increase Clarence (D.W.'s grandfather) had started Clarence Potteries years ago when most of West End was farm land or pasture. In the small, dingy factory, shadowed by Fort York Mountain, he worked beside cheap immigrant labour seven days a week producing simple but classic ceramic plates, dishes, bowls, platters and pots for the Ontario market. Business flourished. The next Clarence, as industrious and tight-fisted as his father, expanded with even more success. There was hardly a house within a two-hundred-mile radius that didn't harbour a Clarence container of some sort. The day D.W. became president, he began spending the fruits of his frugal ancestors. For one thing, he built the Mayfair Crescent house.

Architecturally designed in the not-too-homey Regency style of the early 1900s, it was small as mansions go, but still a mansion; three floors, sixteen rooms,

five bathrooms, six fireplaces and a separate, heated,
triple garage. The well-manicured front lawn, rock
gardens, flagstone walk and wide red gravel driveway
all sloped gracefully from house to street. Behind the
building, the land dropped more steeply and unevenly
until it merged with West Woods, a part of Coote's
Paradise. At the edge of the trees stood a small greenhouse. A pool took up three quarters of its interior. It
had no heater, filter or diving board and could only be
used comfortably on warm clear days when sunlight
filtered through the high Dutch elms and dodged the
opaque bird droppings on the glass-walled structure.
Nevertheless, in polite conversations with the
Clarences, it constituted a bona fide, in-ground swimming pool. The remaining quarter of the greenhouse
was partially closed in, ideal for homemade wine storage.

Mr and Mrs D.W. Clarence had lived in the house
for twenty-five childless years, contributing as little as
possible to business or society. The couple owned two
spoiled Pomeranians. D.W. walked them every night
at ten o'clock, rain or shine.

●　●　●

"It's the first one on your left," Jake said from the back
seat of Wan Ho's squad car. "The one with the lights
on."

They had driven past the university and were
heading back around the loop. Tretheway had used
the time to discuss high spots in *The Tower of London*.
Wan Ho turned left through the open wrought-iron
gates and up the driveway. The tires crunched on the

gravel as he slowed to a stop. Wan Ho jumped out of the car with Jake close behind.

"Very impressive," Wan Ho said, studying the imposing façade of the Clarence house.

"And big," Jake said.

Tretheway grunted, noisily uprooting himself from the poorly sprung passenger seat. He sweated freely. The day had been humid and darkness had brought no relief. High clouds formed. Leaves hung motionless, upside down, asking for rain.

"Let's get in there," Tretheway said. "I think they're waiting for us."

He could clearly see Mrs Clarence in the well-lit living room, glowering through the leaded casement windows at the three of them. A maid stood in the background wringing her hands. After introducing themselves through the locked screen door, the trio was ushered inside where Mrs Clarence repeated her story in more detail.

"But his face, Mrs Clarence," Tretheway asked when she had finished. "You say you didn't see his face."

"No," Mrs Clarence said emphatically. She made untidy waving motions around her face. "His hair was all over. Adele saw him."

Tretheway glanced at the maid. She nodded her head vigorously.

"But you did say him," Tretheway said to Mrs Clarence. "A man."

"Yes." This time not so emphatically.

Tretheway grunted. "What was he wearing?"

"Black, nondescript clothing. He was bent over. Horribly deformed." Mrs Clarence shuddered. "He limped when he ran away."

"Perhaps we should look outside," Wan Ho suggested.

"Right," Tretheway agreed.

"I'm sure the prowler will be gone by now," Jake assured Mrs Clarence.

"I'm more worried about D.W. My husband. He should be back by now."

"Let's have a look," Tretheway said.

On their way to the back door, Mrs Clarence showed them where she had first seen the prowler. "He was right there." She pointed out the window. "You can see where he put the bottle."

Tretheway led the way onto the spacious back porch. He squatted down and examined the bottle without touching it.

"*A Product of Madeira*. Malmsey Wine," he read aloud. "Is your husband by any chance into wine-making?" He hoped for a No.

"Why, yes."

Tretheway straightened up. "On the premises?"

"There are three vats by the swimming pool. In the greenhouse."

"Do you suppose it's Malmsey wine?" Jake asked Tretheway.

"Why do you ask?" Mrs Clarence said.

"I don't think it matters," Tretheway said to Jake. "He's made his point again."

"Who's made his point?" Mrs Clarence said.

"Listen." The maid spoke for the first time.

"What?" Mrs Clarence said.

No one spoke or moved. A beginning hot breeze rustled the leaves. Crickets chirped. A streetcar bell clanged blocks away. Then a dog barked, or really yapped.

"It's Mr Moto," Mrs Clarence said.

"Or Popsie," the maid said.

"Who?" Tretheway asked.

"It's our dogs," Mrs Clarence said. "Down there." She pointed to the barely discernible greenhouse on the edge of light, where the cut grass merged with the natural ravine.

"Sergeant," Tretheway ordered. "You stay with the ladies." He started off the porch.

"Shouldn't we call for another car?" Jake asked.

The ladies looked alarmed. Tretheway glared at Jake. "Not just yet." Then he smiled at Mrs Clarence. "The Constable and I can handle a simple prowler." He turned back to Jake. "Gimme the flashlight."

Jake handed his boss the three cell lantern, thankful he had remembered it.

Wan Ho stayed on the porch and watched the wavering light as Tretheway and Jake carefully trod down the sloping sward, their shadows growing grotesquely toward the darkness. The feeble moonlight outlined the shape of the greenhouse. It appeared much smaller and less picturesque up close. The peeling paint of the metal frame and the filthy glass showed up even at night. Close to the only entrance, they found Mr Moto and Popsie. The dogs were growling over something on the ground. Tretheway pushed the dogs apart roughly with his heavy police boot. "Get away." He considered any dog under twenty pounds untrustworthy. They stopped growling.

"What is it?" asked Jake.

Tretheway shone the light on the objects the dogs had been quarreling over. The crown glittered with reflections while the black woolly hairpiece absorbed most of the illumination.

"I'll wager they belong to Richard III," Tretheway said.

Jake reached down to pick them up, then thought better of it. He looked at Tretheway.

Tretheway shook his head. "Leave them for Wan Ho," he said. "We'd better get in there."

"Right," Jake said.

Tretheway pulled open the door of the greenhouse. The dogs scampered in and started barking again.

Inside, the damp smell of stale, chlorinated water wrinkled both their noses. Tretheway bounced the light around the interior. Wet stains spotted the narrow ledge bordering the pool. Water dripped somewhere. A tall rack containing half grown annual seedlings stood in one corner beside several carelessly stacked garden tools. There were no chairs.

"Sure ain't Hollywood," Jake said.

Tretheway tried a light switch on the wall. Nothing happened. "Great."

He looked back at the main house. Even through the mottled windows of the greenhouse Tretheway could make out Wan Ho on the back porch. The detective stood in a circle of yellow light, hand shielding his eyes, like some ancient sailor in search of whales, peering into the darkness that had swallowed his two colleagues. His charges huddled behind him.

Tretheway focused the flashlight on the rear of the structure. A low wall separated the pool from three metal banded, large oaken casks. They were covered. An arrangement of blinds assured light control for the product. The dogs continued barking.

Tretheway and Jake exchanged nods without speaking. They skirted the pool carefully. Tretheway stopped in front of the first barrel. "Get the light." He pointed with the flashlight at the ceiling.

Jake grasped a piece of string hanging from an overhead exposed light bulb and jerked forty watts into life. The dogs' barking lowered to growls. Tretheway had little trouble lifing the heavy circular lid from the cask. A stench of fermenting grapes over-powered the chemical smell of the pool. The weak light showed foaming wine to the barrel's brim. Bubbles and numerous grapes floated on the disturbed surface.

"Nothing here," Tretheway said.

Jake hesitated. "You sure?" He looked around. "Shouldn't we poke a rake or hoe handle into it?"

"I think not. If there was anything there we'd see it."

Tretheway went on to the next barrel. It took longer than the first but he finally one-handed the awkward lid upwards. More fermenting grape fumes.

"You could get high just smelling this stuff,"

The contents resembled those of the first barrel.

Tretheway pointed to the third one. "Two down."

"One to go," Jake stammered.

Tretheway yanked at the last lid. It didn't budge. He put the flashlight in his pocket and tried again with both hands to no avail. "It's stuck. Gimme a hand."

Jake went to the opposite side of the barrel. They both pulled. Still nothing budged.

"Must be the suction," Jake said.

"Get over here," Tretheway ordered.

Jake moved over beside his boss. The two wrapped their hands around the ample handle. Beside Trethe-way's hands, Jake's looked juvenile.

"Okay," Tretheway said. "On three."

Jake braced himself.

"One, two . . ."

On *three,* they heaved together. A wet, lip-smacking whooshing sound, not unlike a giant drain unclogging, rent the small interior of the greenhouse. The barrel rocked, sloshing homemade wine over its sides. Tretheway and Jake stumbled backwards holding the unstuck lid between them. The dogs ran away yelping.

Edging forward, Tretheway peered apprehensively into the barrel, its contents still eddying from side to side. Jake peeked around his boss's shoulder. What first appeared to be a melon bobbing in a sea of grapes turned out to be the head of D.W. Clarence facing upwards, floating aimlessly, eyes mercifully closed. On either side, his hands rose out of the murky liquid, fingers crooked, palms up, in what must have been one last futile attempt to unseat the jammed lid. Grapes riding in the swishing wine swam in and out of his mouth which was locked open as if in a final bubbly scream.

"Gawd," Jake said.

"I think King Richard has murdered the Duke of Clarence," Tretheway said.

He replaced the lid. The dogs returned, whimpering. Outside the wind rose.

● ● ●

The rest of Sunday night/Monday morning passed in a busy blur. Black and white cruisers, unmarked detective cars, a Black Maria with extra uniforms and a *FY Expo* press car crowded into the Clarence's roomy driveway behind Jake's Pontiac. Doc Nooner arrived in his FY Coroner's black panel truck with Nurse Lodestone driving. Zulp came last with customary sirens. He took charge immediately. A search began.

Uniforms and plainclothesmen alike combed the area around the Clarence house, including part of the woods. Men followed the slippery tortuous trails or crashed through the underbrush where there were no paths. They hunted into the wet bottom land of the ravine where riled swarms of mosquitoes attacked them and the swampy creek bed soaked their feet, in some instances siphoning off their heavy boots.

Zulp had set up the Clarences' outer kitchen as his command post. The generous-sized muddy footprints of reporting policemen soon covered the hardwood floors. Fortunately Mrs Clarence wasn't there. After a brief question period, which revealed nothing new, she and her maid had retired. Mrs Clarence lay now on the luxurious queen-size bed in her own bedroom. Nurse Lodestone watched over her sedated rest. An exhausted Mr Moto and Popsie snored and snuffled on the satin bedspread beside their mistress.

In the small greenhouse, activity occurred in relays. Zulp had already been and gone. Wan Ho had made his examination. Now two burly ambulance attendants moved the offending barrel off to one side. One half-tipped the cask as the other extricated the sodden body of D.W. Clarence, spilling most of the fermented wine over himself and the floor. Some splashed onto the baggy pants and dress shoes of Doc Nooner.

"Sorry, Doc," one attendant said.

"I've had worse," Doc Nooner replied.

"At least you can't smell the chlorine any more," the other attendant said.

They wrestled D.W. onto a waiting stretcher. Doc Nooner bent over and studied the body as best he could under the conditions. He took only minutes.

"Take him to the shop," he told the attendants. "Can't do any more here."

The doctor pushed and excused himself past several detectives dusting for fingerprints on obvious handholds around the pool.

"Any luck?" he asked one of them.

The detective shook his head. "Nothing yet."

Outside the greenhouse, Doc Nooner had to walk by the *Expo* reporter and photographer who stood sullenly together.

"What's going on, Doc?" the reporter asked.

The photographer's speed graphic flashed. Doc Nooner jumped.

"They won't let us in," the reporter said.

"Say we make them nervous," the photographer said.

"No kidding." Doc Nooner rubbed his eyes. He continued up the incline toward the main house following an irregular path already made by police boots in the soft lawn. In the outer kitchen he found Chief Zulp, head in hands, listening to Tretheway finish his *Tower of London* theory. Jake and Wan Ho stood off to one side.

Zulp looked up at Doc Nooner's arrival. "Well?" he said.

"Can't tell 'til we cut him up," Doc Nooner said.

Jake winced.

"But I'd say offhand death by drowning. Looks like someone shut him up in the full barrel."

"Drowned in Malmsey wine?" Wan Ho asked.

"I don't think it's Malmsey," Tretheway said.

"But it was Malmsey in the movie," Jake said.

"And the Malmsey bottle on the porch," Wan Ho said.

"If it had been Malmsey wine in the barrel," Tretheway explained, "he wouldn't've needed the bottle to make his point."

"I see," Zulp said. It was obvious from his expression that he didn't see.

"What the hell is everyone talking about?" Doc Nooner asked.

"Did you see *The Tower of London*?" Tretheway asked. Nooner shook his head.

"Richard III . . ." Tretheway began.

"Just a moment." Zulp stood up. "I'll take it from there. Get it straight in my own mind." This was true, but Zulp also thought he was losing control of the meeting. He clasped his workingman's hands behind him. "This has to do with Tretheway's movie theory. I've heard them all. The horse, the big bird, wicked witch, *Gunga Din* and the French army thing." He rose up and down on the balls of his feet a few times. "Now I'm not saying I accept this theory completely. Serious flaws. Flights of fancy."

Tretheway stared straight ahead.

Zulp unclasped his hands. He lowered his eyes. A tired look passed over his weathered features. "But we don't have anything else," he said quietly. "Just these dumb movies."

No one spoke. Outside sounds intruded. Police-men's boots clomped up and down the porch steps. A vehicle crunched out of the driveway. Muffled shouts came from those still searching.

"*The Tower of London,*" Tretheway prompted.

"Right." Zulp looked up. He pushed his lower lip out. One hand played with the loose folds of skin under his chin. "In *The Tower of London* Richard III murdered a number of people. For the throne. Including the Duke of Clarence. Drowned him. In a vat of Malmsey wine." He glanced at Tretheway before continuing. Tretheway nodded. "Now. The theory is that our perpetrator saw this movie. Got inspired. Picked someone called Clarence. Secluded area. Wore a crown. Pretended to be a cripple. Hunchback. Left the Malm–sey wine bottle. And you know the rest." Zulp looked at Tretheway again.

"Couldn't've done better myself," Tretheway said. Zulp smiled.

"Just a minute," Doc Nooner said. "Where would he get a crown?"

"Military museum," Tretheway said.

"Remember the robbery?" Wan Ho asked Nooner.

"Horsborough'll be glad to get it back," Jake said.

"But what about the wine?" Doc Nooner persisted.

"Don't you find it rather fortuitous that D.W. Clarence was a winemaker?"

"Not really," Tretheway said. "I make wine. You make wine. I'll bet half the people running around these grounds make wine. And suppose he didn't. Then our Fan goes on to another Clarence. Or someone called Duke. Or even another movie."

"You mean he just picks these movies arbitrarily?

And the people?" Nooner asked. "No rhyme or reason?"

"I think so," Tretheway said. "At least so far."

"But why?"

"I don't know."

Doc Nooner shook his head. "You're telling me there's no motive?"

"I didn't say that. I think there's a very strong, powerful motive driving our Fan."

"Oh?"

Everyone looked at Tretheway.

"We just don't know what it is."

"Dammit, Tretheway," Zulp spluttered.

"Hear me out, Chief." Tretheway held up his hand. "In your words, we don't have much else."

Zulp grumbled, but stopped spluttering.

"I think the murders and even the pranks are all camouflage. Red herring country. Bewilderment time. The Fan has the freedom to pick any victim and any movie and meld the two together because he's not bound by any motive." Tretheway spoke to Wan Ho. "I'll wager you've found no connections between the victims?"

"Not really," Wan Ho admitted.

"I mean, they're not all Orangemen? Or streetcar conductors? Electricians? They're not related? Or have the same hobby?"

Wan Ho shook his head.

"And the films are also picked out of the air," Tretheway went on. "No common link. They're chosen to suit the circumstances. To suit the Fan." He began pacing around the kitchen. Everyone waited. He stopped at the screen door and stared out. In the distance, flashlights of the searching policemen resembled giant fireflies flitting erratically in the hazy darkness.

"However," Tretheway said to the night, "that's all going to change." He turned from the door. "If I were a betting man, I'd say the next movie will be the climax. The finale. A golden opportunity for us to catch him."

"Why will this one be different?" Wan Ho asked.

"Because this one will have a motive," Tretheway answered. "I still don't know what. It's almost irrelevant. The important thing is, that this time the Fan will not have the freedom of choice. For anything. I'm convinced the next victim was chosen months, maybe even years ago. And the movie picked out well ahead of time. The others," he waved his big hands in the air, "all leading up to the biggy. He's locked in."

"But we still don't know why?" Zulp asked.

"Not yet," Tretheway said.

"Or who the victim is?" Wan Ho asked.

"No."

"Or the Fan?" Jake asked.

"No."

"And we don't even know what movie," Zulp said.

"On that I can make an educated guess," Tretheway said.

Everyone looked at him again.

"Well?" Zulp said.

"With your permission, Chief," Tretheway said. "I'd like to suggest a meeting. At our place. It's important. Just to set the stage."

"When?" Zulp asked.

Tretheway checked the single digit Bank Of Commerce calendar hanging in the Clarences' kitchen. "Today's the ninth. How about next Sunday? The sixteenth?"

"Why always Sunday?" Zulp asked. His favourite radio show broadcast on Sunday night.

"Because I want to invite Freeman Thake and his West End crew," Tretheway explained. "That's their only night off."

Zulp grumbled. "Anyone else?"

Tretheway looked around the room. "Everyone here. And anyone who goes to the movies with us. Like Terminus and Gum. We'd better include Horsborough. And of course Addie."

"Then we can discuss your educated guess?" Wan Ho said.

"Or anyone's," Tretheway answered.

Zulp brightened. "Sort of a pick-your-movie night?"

Tretheway frowned. "Sort of."

"Good thinking." Zulp jumped up. "That's it, then. Back to work. Promised the boys some pictures. Your Chief-in-action kind of thing. We protect. Seven-thirtyish?"

"What?"

"Next Sunday," Zulp said to Tretheway. "Around half past seven."

"Right," Tretheway said.

Zulp marched outdoors.

Chapter
10

The investigation strengthened Tretheway's theory. No connections surfaced between D.W. Clarence and the other victims or between *The Tower of London* and the other movies. The unharmed crown was returned to a grateful Basil Horsborough and the wig, a commonplace theatrical prop offering no clues, filed in the police lab. No unaccounted fingerprints were found. Thousands of bootprints did nothing but establish a police presence. The prowler escaped. By the time the weekend rolled around, little progress had been made in solving any of the homicides; or, in the coined words of the *FY Expo*, the Movie Murders.

Addie, though balking at the short notice Tretheway had given her, soon jumped enthusiastically into the spirit of the Sunday meeting. She arranged for plenty of fresh bread, three-year-old cheddar cheese, pastrami, corn beef, onion buns, tea, ice, ginger beer (and of course dandelion wine), plus all the nibbles necessary for a successful get-together. Late Sunday afternoon all stood ready. A giant yellow cake (Tretheway's favourite) cooled on the kitchen window sill waiting for a generous slathering of Addie's special yellow icing. Twelve Molson Blue quarts chilled in an ice-filled wash tub on the back porch. Mounds of sandwiches awaited attack on platters with side dishes of lettuce, tomatoes, green onions and radishes plucked from Addie's vegetable patch. Fresh cut flowers from Tretheway's garden filled the common room. Vibrant colours of delphiniums, summer phlox, salvia and snap dragons played background to the heady bouquet of nicotiana and crushed sassafrass leaves. A misleading party ambience prevailed.

The invitees began arriving shortly before Zulp's seven-thirtyish pronouncement. Freeman Thake made the first entrance, a stylish one, wheeling his '38 maroon Buick Roadmaster up the Tretheways' driveway. He'd called for his employees on the way. Lulu Ashcroft and Joshua Pike were picked up together in front of their apartment building where they each rented a bachelor (rumour said they visited often). The two ushers shared the spacious back seat with Neil Heavenly. Violet Farrago sat in the front seat beside her boss offering occasional loud advice about speed limits and stop signs. Addie watched approvingly from the house as Thake spun around the car opening doors for his staff.

Miles Terminus and Bartholemew Gum walked over together. Fred the Labrador followed them into the house. Chief Zulp was chaffeured to the affair in his official, city-crested black limo. "Thank goodness, no sirens," Addie said. Doc Nooner called Wan Ho for a ride at the last minute. Wan Ho had the feeling that the doctor was dodging Nurse Lodestone but said nothing. Basil Horsborough came by bicycle, a black one.

"You've all been briefed about this meeting," Tretheway began.

The murmur of chitchat subsided. Everyone sat comfortably, forming a loose group facing Tretheway in the common room. Some had open stone ginger beer bottles beside them, others had tea or coffee. Large bowls of popcorn or potato chips were placed within reach of all.

"And I'm sure you've heard of Chief Zulp's suggestion about selecting your own movie. Now I know you've heard this at different times. Some later than others. So if you haven't had enough time, don't worry about it. What I'd like to do . . ."

Doc Nooner jumped up. "*Son of Frankenstein*," he interrupted. Most people nodded and smiled.

"Hold it, Doc." Tretheway held both hands out in his all-lanes-stop position.

Doc Nooner sat down.

"What I'd like to do first," Tretheway began again, "is show you how we arrived at our choice. Lead you down the path we followed. Sergeant Wan Ho, Constable Small and I have talked at length about this. Studied it from different angles. And come up with a movie. A logical one." Tretheway paused and studied faces. He hurried back into his explanation when it appeared Zulp was going to ask a question.

"Guideline number one. It must be a spectacular. Not an ordinary movie. A real special. One that would appeal to our Fan's sense of the theatrical. Particularly for a finale. Definitely not a B movie. Two. It must be one that hasn't been shown before. A new movie. Therefore, number three, it must be heavily promoted. Advertised to the point that everyone is aware of the general story line months before it's shown. And number four, it must be shown at the West End."

Freeman Thake stood up. He seemed agitated.

"What is it, Freeman?" Tretheway asked.

"You've just described *Gone with the Wind*," Thake said.

"That's the one," Tretheway said.

"You mean that's the movie you picked?" Zulp said. "The three of you?"

Tretheway nodded.

"Quite a feather in our cap, really," Thake expanded. "Clark Gable and that English girl, Vivien Leigh. One showing only. By invitation. A Saturday evening with an intermission. Then it goes public downtown to a bigger theatre. The Palace, I think."

"By invitation?" Wan Ho repeated.

Thake smiled around the room. "You're all invited."

"What about some other movies?" Zulp asked.

"Okay," Tretheway said. "I know we've set up these guidelines. But they're certainly not etched in copper. If anybody has any suggestions . . ."

Doc Nooner stood up again. "I said *Son of Frankenstein*. All kinds of eerie possibilities. The monster drowned in a sulphur pit. Bela Lugosi as the broken-necked Ygor. Deformed by a hangman. You could do something with all that."

"Good choice, Doc." Tretheway spoke to Jake. "Maybe you'd better write these down."

Addie handed Jake a paper and pencil.

"I've got one," Violet Farrago said. *"The Hunchback of Notre Dame."*

Jake scribbled.

"Charles Laughton as Quasimodo. Looks out for Esmerelda. Real middle ages spooky stuff. Boiling oil and everything."

"Okay Violet," Tretheway acknowledged.

"We have a suggestion," Lulu Ashcroft said. Joshua Pike stood up with her. Tretheway waited while they decided who went first.

"The Cat and the Canary," Lulu said. "Great haunted house stuff. Hands coming out of nowhere. Secret doors. A real screamer."

"And Bob Hope to boot," Joshua said.

By now the rest of the guests were either standing up or raising their hands. Tretheway bent over Jake, ostensibly to read the list.

"Everyone's got their own bloody movie," he whispered.

"Everyone's a critic," Jake said.

Tretheway straightened up. He pointed at Miles Terminus.

"Each Dawn I Die," Terminus said.

"I liked that one," Jake said. "But then, I like James Cagney."

"You also like the Ritz Brothers," Wan Ho said.

"What's wrong with that?"

"They're awful."

"Keep on track," Tretheway said.

"George Raft was good in it too," Terminus went on. "Super prison picture. With its share of murders. Remember when they stabbed the stoolie?"

Jake nodded. Addie handed him another piece of writing paper.

"Okay, Neil," Tretheway said. "You probably see more movies than anyone. What's your professional opinion?"

Neil Heavenly smiled, a young impish grin, no teeth showing. *"The Rains Came,"* he said.

"I almost picked that one myself," Tretheway said.

"Lots of inspiration," Neil elaborated. "Floods. Earthquakes. A monsoon. The Raj, Ranchipur. A sneaky romance with Ty Power as an Indian doctor."

"So you think *The Rains Came* could prod our Fan's imagination?" Tretheway asked.

"Everything from flooding someone's basement to drowning in a shower. Or wait for a real storm," Neil added. "With luck, a hurricane."

"That's all very well," Thake broke in. "But I don't think it has to be a disaster or murder movie."

"I suppose not," Tretheway said. "What's your suggestion?"

"The Story of Vernon and Irene Castle," Thake said.

"You going to dance someone to death, Freeman?" Doc Nooner said.

"Vernon Castle was killed in WWI," Thake said.

"That's right," Jake said. "He was a flyer."

"Doesn't get my vote," Zulp said.

"It was only a suggestion," Thake defended his choice.

"And a very interesting one," Tretheway said.

"*Union Pacific*," Bartholemew Gum said.

"What?" Tretheway looked at Gum.

"That's my movie," Gum explained. "*Union Pacific*. Building a railroad. Gamblers. Gunslingers. Indian attacks. Train crashes. Even romance. Cecil B. DeMille at his finest."

"I think it's a good choice." Jake made more notes. Gum sat down smiling.

"Basil." Tretheway pointed. "We haven't heard from you."

Basil Horsborough mumbled something.

"Can't hear you, Basil," Tretheway said.

"*Tarzan Finds a Son*," Horsborough blurted. "I mean, the Fan could have a picnic with this one. Dress in an animal skin. Swing through the trees in someone's backyard. Even ride an elephant. Don't forget, he stole a horse."

"A little easier to get a horse," Tretheway said.

"But not impossible," Horsborough persisted.

"Well . . . no," Tretheway had to admit.

"Also crocodile wrestling. Nasty white hunters. Guns. And remember Boy caught in that giant tarantula web?" Horsborough clucked. "All grist for the Fan's mill."

Tretheway nodded. "We've got it all written down." He looked around the room. "That about does it."

Zulp coughed.

"Chief, of course," Tretheway said. "Saved the best 'till last."

Zulp stood up. "Haven't given this too much thought. Busy. Lots to do." He stared at the ceiling.

"You have a movie?" Tretheway prompted.

"Haven't seen too many. But there is one. Stands out. Memorable."

Everyone waited. Tretheway found himself leaning forward on his chair with the others.

"The Terror of Tiny Town," Zulp announced.

Tretheway frowned. He exchanged looks with Jake and Wan Ho. They shook their heads.

"You got us there, Chief," Tretheway said.

"A musical Western. Lots of action. Gunfights. Hard riding cowboys. Dynamite. Log cabin exploding."

"A musical?" Wan Ho asked.

"Yes," Zulp said. "Got some catchy numbers."

"Who's in it?" Jake asked.

"That's the interesting part," Zulp said. "The whole cast is midgets."

"Midgets?" Jake repeated.

"Yes," Zulp said. "All little people." A sudden glimmer of uncertainty passed over his wrinkled features.

"Something else?" Wan Ho asked.

"And a penguin," Zulp said. "A giant penguin was in it. I'm not sure why."

"All food for thought, Chief," Tretheway said. "You got that, Jake?"

"I'll remember that one," Jake said.

Zulp sat down, still frowning. Tretheway noticed Addie fidgeting by the kitchen door, a sure sign that sandwich time was not far away. He decided to sum up.

"That's about it, then. There were more suggestions than I anticipated. All imaginative. Some more than others. Thank you for every one of them. But please don't forget *Gone with the Wind*. It's still close to the top of the list. And we'll see it as a group." Tretheway looked at Thake. "Saturday?" Thake nodded. "Seven o'clock sharp."

"Right," Tretheway said. "Think about it. Try to see it through the eyes of the Fan. And if you get any ideas, we can talk about it."

"Does this mean another meeting?" Zulp asked.

"I don't think that's necessary," Tretheway replied.

He spoke to the room. "Individual phone calls would better suit the purpose. Call any one of us." Tretheway indicated himself, Wan Ho and Jake. "Thank you for your patience."

Polite unexpected applause goaded Addie into action. She pushed through the swinging door of the kitchen and returned on the next swing bearing a sandwich-laden tray. Two students followed carrying a punch bowl brimming with a dandelion-wine-and-soda-water mixture and a second tray jammed with a collection of unmatched glasses. Addie announced that other spirits and beer were available in the kitchen on a help-yourself basis.

For most, the meeting changed ·direction. Talk turned to subjects as diverse as Adolph Hitler's actions in Europe to a *FY Expo* article about a man in Denver who couldn't stop walking backwards. Doc Nooner and Gum discussed the punch heard 'round the world in the recent Louis/Galento world championship boxing match. Neil Heavenly described an RFYLI demonstration he'd seen of a new automatic weapon (Bren gun). Lulu Ashcroft and Joshua Pike raised eyebrows bemoaning the price of a new dining room suite ($109, nine piece, walnut) they were going halfers on. Thake complained about the price ($920) of a new Ford V8 he was considering for Mrs. Thake. Violet Farrago defended the economy by spinning around, modelling the dress she had bought for ninety-nine cents. Miles Terminus was full of a bargain funeral he had read about ($120); "and that includes a solid oak casket," he said.

Zulp missed most of this by dodging through people on his way to the door and home. He had made earlier excuses to Addie about getting a good night's sleep for Monday morning but, in truth, his favourite radio program, "American Album of Familiar Music," came on at half past nine.

Fred wandered freely in the crowd begging the equivalent of three sandwiches. Thake's four employees started a Rummy 500 game while their boss explained the social niceties of ballroom dancing to Basil Horsborough. Tretheway, Jake and Wan Ho were the only ones who continued to rehash the movies.

"So we're agreed then," Tretheway said. "*Gone with the Wind* is our best choice."

"The most logical," Jake said.

"What about *The Terror of Tiny Town*?" Wan Ho grinned.

Tretheway shook his head. "I was afraid he was going to ask you to round up all the midgets."

"We got any?" Jake asked.

"I don't know," Wan Ho said.

"We only had seven Indians."

"Your ancestors must have a quotation for this," Jake said.

Wan Ho's brow wrinkled as he mentally flipped through his Charlie Chan aphorism file. "Ah," he said finally. "Each man thinks his own cuckoos better than next man's nightingales."

The three bowed slightly toward each other. Addie pushed among them with a sandwich tray.

"What are you up to?" she asked.

"We're discussing Oriental History," Tretheway said.

"I see your dandelion wine is moving well tonight," Jake said to Addie.

They turned and watched as Freeman Thake spun a protesting Basil Horsborough around in an impromptu demonstration of the fox trot.

"He'll sleep well tonight," Addie said. She went toward the twirling pair with sandwiches.

● ● ●

"You know what bothers me about tonight?" Jake said.

"What's that?" Tretheway drained a Molson quart. Everyone had finally gone home. They were the only ones in the house still up. Jake stood now poised on the back stairs heading for bed. Tretheway sat at the kitchen table.

"Two things, really. One bad, one good," Jake went on. "It's unfortunate the next victim, the killee so to speak, wasn't here. At the meeting. Too bad he couldn't've heard what was said. Be forewarned."

"I assume that's the bad one," Tretheway said.

Jake nodded. "But on the other hand, I'm glad our Fan wasn't here. The killer. But for the opposite reason."

Tretheway stared at Jake. A slow humourless smile spread over his face.

"What's the matter?" Jake asked.

"You're serious, aren't you?"

Jake nodded.

"Jake, I'd bet my pension they were both here. In this house. At the meeting."

Jake's eyes went twice their normal size.

"But it doesn't really change anything," Tretheway said.

"Eh?"

"I mean, you've still got one good one and one bad one."

Jake went up the stairs without saying goodnight.

Chapter

Gone *with the Wind* lived up to its ground-breaking publicity. The audience oohed at the magnificent splendor of the Old South and aahed at the lavish costumes in the opening shots of Tara. They picked their favourites early in the Rhett loves Scarlett, Scarlett loves Ashley, Ashley loves Melanie complicated relationships.

Image followed memorable image; the indifference of Scarlett O'Hara walking through the railway depot where hundreds of Confederate soldiers lay wounded or dying in a moaning panorama, the breath-taking escape of Scarlett and Rhett from burning Atlanta, the madness of Scarlett's father (Thomas Mitchell), the horror of Bonnie's fatal riding accident, the dignity of Hattie MacDaniel contrasted with the "I don't know nothin' bout birthin' babies" mentality of

Prissy (Butterfly McQueen), and the inconsolable re-
morse of Ashley over gentle Melanie's death. Probably
the most memorable scene, Scarlett literally kissed off
her feet before Rhett carries her up the wide red-car-
peted staircase two steps at a time, brought romantic
palpitations to the hearts of the ladies and a matching
surge of macho identification to the breasts of the men.

When Rhett's final, controversial, melting-into the-
fog line, 'Frankly my dear I don't give a DAMN,' ended
the four hour saga, almost everyone stood and ap-
plauded, an unheard-of reaction in the West End Theatre.

Each one of the Tretheway party responded to the
movie in a different way. Tretheway never lost himself in its mood as he would have in another *Four Feathers* or any Sherlock Holmes film. To him it remained
celluloid. Jake became part of the Old South from the
beginning credits but, as Wan Ho said, "You'd do the
same thing with a Three Stooges flick." Addie was
emotionally drained. Lulu and Joshua shed tears, each
at different places. Even hard-nosed Violet cried when
Melanie went to heaven. Doc Nooner paid rapt attention to the hospital scenes, but became bored with the
kissing.

Except for the authentic uniforms, Basil Horsborough didn't enjoy anything after the Civil War. Neil
Heavenly liked everything he managed to see but his
concern centred on the projector and the reels. Miles
Terminus and Gum sat together and, as with Doc, the
love scenes were their least favourite. Zulp sat in a special row of dignitaries beside Mayor Phineas (Fireball)
Trutt. The mayor became noticeably excited during the
fire scene.

●　●　●

Over the next couple of weeks, Tretheway received several interesting phone calls from the group. Once again, he was surprised at the keen response. The Civil War came out on top.

Gum called first to suggest the war itself posed endless possibilities of murder from bullets to sabres to bayonets, among others. Basil Horsborough supposed wildly that despite their vintage someone might try to activate the ship's guns guarding his museum. But how they could be pointed effectively, or how anyone could be inveigled to stand in front of one, taxed his and Tretheway's imagination. Neil Heavenly thought the scene where Scarlett shoots the Union Army deserter in the face with his own firearm could somehow be recreated. It also gave credibility, Neil implied, to the theory of a female killer. The burning of Atlanta garnered favourites, Tretheway among them. Joshua Pike had it at the top of his selections, but when pressed for an explanation couldn't explain. "Just a gut feeling," he said.

Freeman Thake proposed death involving horses, inspired by Mr O'Hara's riding accident. Lulu Ashcroft said the same thing, but her reason came from Bonnie's fall from yet another horse. Doc Nooner insinuated that Melanie's waning strength, resulting in her lingering demise, could have been brought about by injection or poison. His viewpoint was the least popular with Tretheway. Jake and Wan Ho felt that the actual fighting should play a part but neither could recall enough of the surprisingly short montage of battle scenes to argue sensibly.

Tretheway forced himself to remain objective. "Let's keep it open," he said.

Addie abstained. And Zulp gave no suggestions at all for *Gone with the Wind*. He did, however, urge Wan Ho for some action (he didn't say what) on the midget cowboy musical movie.

● ● ●

By the middle of August, Tretheway was disconsolate. He had all the necessary facts within his grasp, in his opinion, to solve the murders, but appeared to be no closer to the solution.

"Doesn't that dog ever go home?" he said.

Fred wagged her tail. She had wandered into the parlour after supper and lay now with her head on the lower shelf of the tea wagon.

Addie looked disapprovingly at her brother. "Albert, what's the matter?"

Tretheway didn't answer. In the background, the canned voice of The Old Ranger was spinning one more tale on the Friday episode of "Death Valley Days." Jake lowered his newspaper.

"You want to talk about it?" he asked his boss.

"We've talked our ears off." Tretheway complained.

"You certainly have." Addie's empty cup and saucer rattled with indignation as she put it back on the tray. Fred lifted her head. "Too much talk. It's time you did something. Get a move on."

Jake hid behind his paper. Tretheway's face reddened. He jerked upright in his soft chair. Cigar ashes sprayed over his shirt front. Just as suddenly, he re-laxed and leaned back.

"You're quite right, Addie," he said. "It *is* time to get a move on. A time for action. Sometimes a decision, right or wrong, is better than none at all." He brushed the ashes from his chest. "If the Fan follows his pattern, something should happen in a week. Maybe two."

"Okay." Jake folded his paper away. He clapped his hands together. "What's the movie?" he asked Tretheway.

"*Gone with the Wind*," Tretheway replied without hesitation.

"And the scene?"

Tretheway hesitated only briefly. "Atlanta," he said. "The burning of Atlanta. A huge raging fire. That would appeal to the Fan. A great climax."

"Where?" Jake pressed. "What's he going to burn down?"

"Something spectacular," Tretheway said.

"Like what?"

"How do I know?" Tretheway's foul mood threatened to return.

"What did they burn down in the movie?" Addie asked.

"An old MGM set," Jake said. "From King Kong."

"But we don't have one of those," Tretheway said.

"I'm just trying to help," Addie said.

"And it was planned. Everybody knew about it," Jake said. "It was all in the script."

"We don't have one of those either," Tretheway said.

No one spoke for a moment. Then Addie cleared her throat unnecessarily. Tretheway looked at her sideways. So did Jake.

"We do in a way," she said quietly. "I know of a fire. A nice big spectacular planned fire."

● ● ●

On December 13, 1889, a meeting was held of those interested in building a railway up the Fort York Mountain (elevation 290') from the head of James Street. A scheme was decided on, a Board of Directors elected and one third of the capital stock of $20,000 subscribed. Thus began the Fort York Incline Railway.

The Incline climbed at a forty-five degree angle on two raised tracks, one for up, one for down, laid on creosote-treated wooden ties. An ingenious steam powered cable system (later electric) allowed the two mirror-image cars to pass each other at the midway point. Each twenty-ton steel car accommodated two horse-and-buggies (later automobiles). Approximately thirty passengers sat on the practical bench seats inside a covered side section. At the mountain's top stood a sturdy, four storey building. It housed a 125 hp engine, living quarters for the engineer and his family, a waiting room and ticket office. Adults or vehicles could take the eighty-second trip up for ten cents, children five cents. Prices dropped for going down. Wooden stairs parallelled the tracks for those who wished to pay nothing up or down.

The Fort York Incline prospered. People flocked up the escarpment to visit restaurants, summer playhouses, wooded parks or the mountain TB sanitorium. They came just to inhale the famous healthy mountain breeze or, when Stelfy wasn't puffing black smoke over FY Harbour, to enjoy the stunning view over Lake Ontario as far as Toronto, forty miles away. Even delivery vehicles and ambulances rode the Incline instead of negotiating the slower, circuitous mountain roads, most in need of paving.

By the thirties however, the blasting of a new mountain access route through the limestone, and the increase of more privately owned, dependable vehicles on the improved roads meant less and less business for the railway. The Fort York Incline withered into bankruptcy. In 1933 the city took it over for back taxes. For the past six years, it had lain unused, rails rusting, ticket office and building deserted, with the two cars, wheels chocked, exposed at the top of the Incline. An adventurous youth out to prove his manhood could occasionally be seen clambering up the deteriorating ties. From a viable transportation service and a tourist attraction, the FY Incline had degenerated into a liability.

Mayor Phineas "Fireball" Trutt came to the rescue; or really, his trustworthy wife Bertha did.

"Give us a lemon," she paraphrased her family motto, "and we'll give you lemonade." Bertha suggested to her husband that, "Rather than spend good city money on labour and machines to tear the structure down, why not burn it down? And if you do," she further suggested, "why not make it an event, a municipal fete, perhaps on a holiday?"

The mayor wasn't the brightest person she had ever lived with, but even he saw the money-saving aspects and electoral showmanship of her idea. And as a bonus, he could don his old firefighter's uniform, with helmet, to safely face once more his loveable enemy, fire. After a quick telephone conference with the Fire Chief and Zulp, he decided on his own authority to call a press conference the next day and announce his surprise spectacular. That evening Bertha Trutt called at least one of her close friends.

● ● ●

Tretheway and Jake stared at Addie.

"They're supposed to announce it tomorrow," she continued.

"Addie," Tretheway said, "what are you talking about?"

"The Fort York Incline. They're going to burn it down. On Labour Day."

"Who's they?" Jake asked.

"Why?" Tretheway asked. "And how do you know all this?"

Addie pulled her crocheting out from behind a sofa cushion and examined the stitches closely. "Bertha Trutt told me." She went on to explain the whole story to her attentive audience.

"I'll be damned," Tretheway said when Addie finished.

"You think we've got our location?" Jake asked.

"I'd say so," Tretheway said. "Now we need the two main characters."

"Any ideas?" Jake said.

"When's Labour Day?" Tretheway side-stepped Jake's question.

"Two weeks Monday," Addie said. "September four."

Tretheway frowned.

"What's the matter?" Jake asked.

"Nothing special." Tretheway heaved himself out of his chair and stepped over to the bookcase. "Didn't we have an encyclopedia?"

"Two volumes," Addie said. "Right in front of your nose."

"They're not very good," Jake said. "Book-of-the-Month Club bonus."

Tretheway plucked both books from the shelf with one hand. He blew dust from their tops. Addie looked away.

"I think I'll go read for a while." Tretheway started out of the parlour, then stopped.

"This theory," he said pretending to examine the encyclopedias, "tieing in the burning of Atlanta to the Fort York Incline. We'll just keep it to ourselves."

"What about Wan Ho?" Jake asked.

Tretheway reconsidered. "He should know."

Addie looked as if she was going to ask a question.

"But no one else," Tretheway said to his sister. "Even Bertha Trutt."

Addie went about her crocheting but nodded imperceptibly. She and Jake heard Tretheway open and close the ice box on his way upstairs. Jake spun the radio dial to "Hollywood Hotel."

●　●　●

Close to midnight, by the end of the overseas news broadcast, Jake assumed his boss was gone for the night. Addie had retired an hour earlier, right after "First Nighter." Jake made the regular rounds of the ground floor checking doors and windows. When he entered the kitchen, Tretheway appeared suddenly and silently from the darkened opening of the back stairs. "Geez!" Jake jumped out of his skin.

"Did you know that Atlanta is the capital of Georgia?" Tretheway waved the AA to Lavca Bay volume of the encyclopedia in the air.

"You scared the hell out of me."

"Did you know it's the biggest city in the state?"

"Not really . . ."

"Or that it's near the Appalachian foothills?"

Jake shook his head.

"How about the transportation centre of the state?"

Jake shook his head again.

"The end of the rail line. Which would make it the terminal, so to speak. And because of this, it wasn't even called Atlanta until 1845. Before that it had another name."

Tretheway paused. Jake waited.

"Terminus."

"Eh?"

"The city of Terminus. The burning of Terminus. Not Atlanta."

"You mean . . ."

Tretheway leaned back against the kitchen counter. A satisfied look spread over his face.

"You mean," Jake tried again, "Miles Terminus?"

Tretheway nodded. "Now we know who. At least, Who Number Two. And we also know when and where."

"Who number two?"

"The victim. Terminus. We don't know who Number One. The killer."

"And we still don't know why."

"Right." Tretheway went to the ice box. "Want to split a quart?"

"Sure," Jake said. He normally didn't take too much liquid before bedtime but with Tretheway's idea of a split, he knew there was little to worry about.

"Let's talk about the why." Tretheway drank from the bottle after filling a small tumbler with ale for Jake. "Let's check into Miles Terminus' background. Look for a motive. The Beach Strip shooting comes to mind."

"Long time ago."

"I know."

"Right," Jake said. "We'd better bring Wan Ho up to date."

Tretheway nodded. "From there it should be a simple matter. Even if we don't know who Number One is yet. Just stay alert. And keep an eye on Terminus." He frowned at the wall calendar.

Jake sensed an aura of uncertainty around his boss. "Something still troubling you?"

Tretheway didn't answer right away. Annoying elusive doubts nibbled at his confidence. "We've got two weeks." He took a long pull of Blue. "Let's think about it."

● ● ●

On Saturday, August 19, as Addie had foretold, Mayor Trutt announced the burning of Fort York's Incline Railway to celebrate the Labour Day holiday. The media were impressed. His unprepared colleagues on city council were not.

On the following Monday Tretheway, with Jake in attendance, laid out all his surprises, guesses, conclusions and plans before Wan Ho in the privacy of his office. Although it went against the bureaucratic system, he had decided not to inform Chief Zulp until later. Wan Ho agreed. For the next few days, a pair of Wan Ho's most trusted detectives looked into the affairs and background of Miles Terminus.

In any investigation of the retired police officer, it was impossible to overlook the 1919 shooting incident that had plagued his career. The police file dutifully noted: "FY Beach Strip, 2:10 a.m., Monday June 16, Constable M. Terminus in defense of his own life shot and killed one Vincent Paradiso, burglar." Terminus's own neatly handwritten version followed. A copy of Paradiso's criminal record was stapled to the file folder along with a Police Commissioner's letterhead explaining Terminus's exoneration. Almost as an afterthought, a smaller piece of notepaper listed Paradiso's survivors: two children, a boy, twelve, and a girl, nine.

Wan Ho's men pursued the cold trail as best they could through an orphanage and a string of foster homes. They got back to Wan Ho late Thursday. He appeared in Tretheway's office Friday morning.

"So the children can't be found?" Tretheway said at the end of Wan Ho's record.

"Not likely," Wan Ho said.

"Or traced in any way?" Tretheway persisted.

"No. Virtually impossible," Wan Ho said. "Certainly not by Labour Day."

"Doesn't someone keep a record of these kids?" Jake asked.

"Only until they're sixteen," Wan Ho answered. "Hell. We're talking twenty years ago." He looked at Tretheway. "Is this important?"

"Could be. It could become a piece of the puzzle." Tretheway leaned back in his creaking chair. "Anything else turn up?"

"No," Wan Ho said. "Our Terminus led a pretty clean life."

"I'm not surprised," Tretheway said.

"Should we tell Miles?" Jake asked.

"Yes," Tretheway said. "He should know what's going on."

"What about Zulp?" Wan Ho asked.

"Him too," Tretheway said. "But not today. For either of them. There'll be time enough to tell them Monday." He swivelled his chair to face the window. Pedestrians shuffled past on the sixth day of the heat wave. Cars drove by at the speed limit or below. In the corner, a standup fan whirred ineffectively. "It's like a huge jigsaw puzzle. We're close to finishing. But there's still pieces missing. Out there somewhere. Under a serviette. Or on the floor. Maybe another's in backwards. Or maybe the dog ate one." Tretheway continued to stare out the window.

Jake and Wan Ho exchanged disquieting looks, then slipped noiselessly out of the office.

Chapter

12

Saturday evening passed quietly at the Tretheways'. A pick-up euchre game began about eight o'clock with Tretheway and Jake pitted against Gum and Wan Ho. Miles Terminus looked on. Wan Ho had brought the uninformed Terminus over, ostensibly for a social evening at the Tretheways', but knowing glances had been exchanged among Tretheway, Jake and Wan Ho when they arrived. Surveillance, however, was still light. The last summer holiday lay a distant nine days away.

In the back yard, weak moonlight highlighted the motionless boughs of the maples and pines drooping in the heavy air. Cicadas buzzed noisily. Fred sprawled on the cool flagstone patio, her head squidged up against the double screen doors leading to the common room. Wet nose prints covered the lower glass sections.

Tretheway played cards indifferently for about an hour. Then he excused himself and, giving no reason, carried his ale and cheese sandwich with onion down the hall into the parlour. Addie took his place in the euchre game.

"You'll have to forgive Albert," she said to the table. "He's got a lot on his mind."

Later in the evening when Addie played a lone hand, Jake sauntered down the hall and peeked into the parlour. Tretheway sat in his large chair reading a red, leather-bound volume that Jake recognized as part of a Shakespeare tragedy set. Thick smoke rings hung over his head. A Blue stood reassuringly close. Someone had taken pity on Fred and let her in the house. She lay on the marble hearth beside Tretheway's empty sandwich plate. Jake stifled an impulse to speak. He returned to the card game. Addie looked at him questioningly.

"He's reading," Jake said.

"Shakespeare?" Addie asked.

Jake nodded. "*Hamlet*."

"Just leave him be."

●　●　●

The evening wound up early. Gum left first, followed closely by Wan Ho with Terminus discreetly in tow. Addie washed up in the kitchen and went to her bed. None of them said good night to Tretheway. Jake poked his head between the parlour doors and spoke to his boss.

"Want me to lock up?"

Tretheway grunted without looking up from his

book. Fred padded over to Jake. Jake assumed that the grunt meant Tretheway would lock up when he was ready.

"Want me to send the dog home?" Jake tried again.

Tretheway didn't even grunt. Jake eased himself away and went back into the empty common room. Fred followed.

"You go home now, Fred." Jake pushed the dog by her soft rump out through the French doors. Fred looked back over her shoulder, then loped toward the dark neighbouring yard and her own doghouse. Jake went upstairs.

Despite open windows, the humid air moved hardly at all in the close upper floors of the old house. Jake thought he'd never get to sleep, but lay only minutes before the mesmerizing spin of the window fan and his general contentment with life combined to push him gently into the Land of Nod, the world of dreams.

Across a verdant fairway, a dozen maidens cavorted, leapt and pirouetted in full colour clad only in golf bags. Vivaldi music swelled. Jake struck pure shot after pure shot to the centre of a velvety green the colour of backlit emeralds.

"Jake! Wake up!"

The earth quaked. Grass covered knolls heaved. Maidens toppled. Bunkers collapsed. Jake's shots became errant. "Find shelter!" He sat up.

"Open your eyes," Tretheway said.

When Jake did open his eyes, a blurry vision of Tretheway sitting on the edge of his sagging mattress confronted him.

"Are you awake?" the vision asked him.

"Eh?"

"Go stick your head under the tap," Tretheway said.

Jake stumbled into the bathroom. The head that stared back at him from the medicine cabinet reflected thinning hair standing in unruly spikes, an untidy moustache and bloodshot eyes, caked with sleep, blinking in a wet face. But he was mostly awake.

Back in the bedroom still towelling himself off, Jake picked up his watch from the side table. The hands showed twenty-five minutes past two.

"Do you know what time it is?" he said.

"Yes." Tretheway indicated that Jake should sit down. "Hear me out."

Jake sat on the bed. Tretheway began pacing the bedroom carpet.

"The when is wrong," he said.

"What?"

"It's not going to happen on Labour Day. Too many people. Police. Firemen. There'll be more security than the King and Queen had."

"So when . . . ?"

"Any suitable night between now and the holiday. Probably on a weekend."

Jake thought for a moment. "So you're talking next Saturday? Or Sunday?"

"Or tonight."

"Tonight?"

"That's why I woke you up."

Jake stared at his boss. He was now fully awake.

"Let's get over there," Tretheway ordered.

"Where?"

"The Fort York Incline."

"Now?"

"This very minute."

"But . . ."

"One more thing," Tretheway said. "I called Terminus. There's no answer."

Jake shivered in the sticky air.

"I'll call Wan Ho while you get dressed."

Tretheway went downstairs.

Minutes later Jake joined his boss in the front hall. Tretheway had just hung up the phone.

"How sure are you about tonight?" Jake asked.

"Enough to ask Wan Ho to join us."

"What about the fire department?"

"Not that sure," Tretheway snapped.

"Just asking." Jake went out the door.

Hot air blew around and over the windshield into their faces as Jake wheeled his heavy '33 Pontiac across the dark city. He had hurriedly put the top down before they had taken off. They passed or saw no one.

"You want to go to the top or bottom?" Jake shouted.

"The bottom," Tretheway shouted back.

Jake headed up James Street to the mountain's base. The hard rubber tires bumped over the rutted ground as he turned into the parking lot at the foot of the Incline and parked beside two derelict vehicles and an older pickup truck. He turned the engine off. Sounds obscured by the straight eight's deep-throated rumble now intruded on the silence; night creatures skittering through the underbrush, the everpresent chorus of heat-loving cicadas, steel slag hissing into FY

Harbour, distant highway traffic and overall, the birth of a wind, still unrefreshing, sighing through the tree-tops.

Tretheway and Jake got out of the car. Their gaze swept the Incline's spidery latticework as it rose steeply on its steel trellis to the mountaintop, to where the abandoned engineering building loomed blackly against the lighter sky. Clouds formed overhead.

"See anything?" Jake asked.

"No." Tretheway squinted into the night. "Although . . ."

"What?"

"Could be a shadow." Tretheway pointed upwards. "About halfway up."

Jake stared along his boss's arm. "Can't make it out."

"Let's get up there."

"How?"

"Walk up the tracks."

"But they're open," Jake protested. "There are big spaces between the ties."

Tretheway started through the crumbling archway leading to the tracks.

"And it must get to forty, fifty feet in the air," Jake shouted after Tretheway.

"Bring the flashlight," Tretheway ordered.

Jake hustled around to the back of the Pontiac. He yanked open the rumble seat. Leaning into the dark hole, he fumbled through the bric-a-brac on the floor— screwdriver, scout knife, a local unfolded map, a wrench, an old sweater, oil can—until his hand closed round the familiar flashlight. As an afterthought, he slipped the knife into his pocket, and he ran after his boss.

Chapter Twelve

Tretheway began his ascent, confidently taking the uniformly spaced ties two at a time. Jake found the spacing awkward. For him two ties at once demanded an unsafe long stride, while taking them singly produced a quick mincing pace. And to walk on the rails required too delicate a balancing act.

"I hope there's no electricity left in these," Jake said.

Tretheway kept climbing. Jake noticed the shadowy shapes on the ground getting smaller and smaller. The spaces between the ties were not quite large enough for a body to fit through, but between the up-and-down tracks the ties didn't always meet, leaving random uneven gaps, some large enough for a person even of Tretheway's girth to plummet through. Partway up Tretheway stumbled and went down on one knee.

"Be careful," Jake said.

"What's that smell?" Tretheway ran a finger along a tie and held it under his nose.

"Probably old creosote," Jake said.

"How about new gasoline?" Tretheway said.

"Maybe we should call . . ."

"C'mon."

The two of them climbed cautiously toward the suspicious shadow that Tretheway had seen from below. Six-foot-high braced stakes stood at fifty-foot intervals between the two tracks. They supported lights, now disconnected, old cables and reflectors. The one they now approached appeared much thicker than the others.

"Can you see anything?" Jake asked. He was several ties behind Tretheway.

"I think it's someone tied to the post."

Jake shined his flashlight at the shadows. "Can you make out who?"

"Could be Terminus."

Jake forced himself to ask. "As in the burning of Terminus?"

Before Tretheway could answer, a muffled explosion, a low roar, then crackling came from below. Their heads jerked toward the sounds. At fifty feet above the ground they were far enough away from the base to watch the perspective of the inverted V of the tracks disappear into a miniature horizontal line of flame. The freshening northeast wind sweeping in from the harbour fanned the flames and encouraged their spread upwards.

"Look!" Jake said pointing.

"I can see."

"No," Jake said pointing again. "The parking lot."

Two pinpricks of white light indicated a vehicle, from this distance about the size of a Dinky Toy, maneuvering erratically in the parking lot. Gears clashed, tires squealed, then red tail lights faded away as it roared up the mountain road.

"Must be that pickup," Tretheway said.

"Do you suppose that's . . ." Jake looked at Tretheway.

"I'm sure of it."

Tretheway stepped toward the post, quicker now, not as carefully as before. His right leg disappeared into one of the irregular spaces. He sat down heavily, his other leg shooting out in front of him. His thick muscular thigh, jammed between two of the ties, saved him from painful injury. "Damn!"

"What's the matter?"

"I'm stuck."

For the next few minutes, which seemed like hours to both of them, Jake put his arms underneath Tretheway's armpits and, risking hernia, pulled in jerks while his boss strained upwards. Jake looked over his shoulder. The flames were closer or higher, he couldn't tell which, but were definitely noisier. It took six precious minutes before Tretheway's upper leg slithered out of the wooden pincers.

"You okay?" Jake asked.

Tretheway checked his leg. His pants were torn and stained, but except for a tingling sensation in his foot, he felt all right.

"My foot's asleep."

"Can you walk?"

"Have to." Tretheway stood up unsteadily.

The oil-soaked wood sizzled in the flames. They could feel the heat of the fire. Moans came from the shadowy stake. Jake stepped the rest of the way almost carelessly.

"It is Miles," he shouted.

Tretheway limped up behind. "How is he?"

Terminus groaned louder. His eyes were closed. He had been bound hand and foot and gagged before being tied to the stake. Jake's flashlight revealed several nasty welts on his head. One in particular, caked with dried blood, ran at an angle from just above his ear to his chin. Terminus's eyelids flickered.

"At least he's alive." Jake struggled with the gag.

"Is he conscious?" Tretheway asked.

Miles Terminus opened his eyes wide, terrified. His mouth worked, silently at first. Then he spoke.

"He hit me."

"What?" Jake said.

"With his sword."

"Who hit you?" Tretheway asked.

"General Sherman."

Tretheway and Jake looked at each other.

"He's on Strange Street," Jake said.

"Let's get him out of here." Tretheway took the flashlight from Jake. It looked like a penlight in his giant hand. "Untie him."

Jake fumbled with the rope. "I can't undo the damn knots." His voice rose.

"Take it easy," Tretheway said. He looked back down the tracks. Thunder rumbled. The wind, stronger now, pushed the flames relentlessly higher. Smoke stung their eyes.

"Do you have a knife?" Tretheway asked.

"No." Jake worked on one of the larger knots. "Yes!" he shouted, remembering the scout knife. He dug it out of his pocket. His hands shook.

Tretheway grabbed him firmly by the arm. He shined the flashlight on the unopened knife in Jake's grip. "Jake," he said slowly and distinctly. "Open it carefully. Don't drop it."

Jake's breathing slowed. He unfolded the knife blade deliberately. The phony imitation ivory handle, with its picture of Baden Powell, felt comfortable in his palm.

"Now cut," Tretheway said. He jammed the flashlight in his pocket.

Two beams of light swept over the top of the Incline.

"What's that?" Jake asked.

"Could be headlights."

"Maybe Wan Ho."

"Let's hope so."

"What if it's . . . ?"

"Keep cutting."

The scout knife had seen sharper days. Jake sawed at the tough hemp of Terminus's bindings while Tretheway pulled them taut. Several gave way. Invasive, out-of-place metallic clangs came from the top of the Incline; then a low but shrill metal squeal. Jake looked a question at Tretheway but kept sawing. Tretheway paid no attention to the noises.

"I'm getting hot," Terminus said.

"Just another minute, Miles," Tretheway soothed.

The metallic clangs grew louder. A high-pitched metal-on-metal squeal overlapped a tongue-biting metallic screech they couldn't ignore. Tretheway looked up. A large ominous silhouette gradually moved into his view at the top of the hill. The squeals continued.

It took Tretheway seconds to respond.

"Good God! It's one of the railway cars."

"Eh?" Jake stopped cutting.

"There!" Tretheway shouted at the left hand track.

"It's moving!" Jake shouted back.

Tretheway glared into the darkness. He could feel the heat on the back of his neck. A small-scale figure climbed onto the roof of the Incline car and disappeared inside. The heavy coach slowly, ever so slowly, overcame its inertia and began its squealing descent down the rusty tracks toward the three stunned policemen.

Jake needed no urging to double his efforts. Tretheway tore apart a couple more weakened strands. Smoke enveloped them. The fire reached blistering heat. Tretheway figured they had less than a minute. The knife blade broke. Jake stared at the useless handle, then at Tretheway. He remembered afterward, that this was when the slow motion started.

In a Herculean effort supercharged by life-saving adrenalin, Tretheway took a firm handhold near the top of the stake, wedged his size thirteens between two ties and using his strong leg muscles developed over years of competetive hammer-throwing plus his formidable weight, pulled the upright toward him until it formed almost a quarter circle, Terminus bending easily with it. The noise it made when the base snapped off sounded like the cracking of a Brobdignagian bull whip. Tretheway and Terminus toppled over backwards, fortunately uphill away from the fire and, also fortunately, close to but not through one of the gaps in the ties.

At the same instant the railway car blurred past. The old coach without gears, brakes, cables or the natural counterweight of the companion car to hold it back, had quickly reached an alarming speed. It threatened to jump track.

General Sherman braced himself in the open section of the coach and leaned recklessly over the guard rail flailing his 1853 Pattern cavalry sword. The double-breasted, dark blue frock coat, with blue velvet collar and cuffs, came to his knees. Light from the fire flickered over the two rows of shiny breast buttons grouped in threes. Shoulder straps with two stars denoted the rank of Major General.

The fire roared. A whirlwind of sparks engulfed the front of the coach. Metal shrieks came from its protesting undercarriage. Lightning flashed simultaneously with an ear-shattering crash of thunder.

The whole structure vibrated. But the scariest, most noticeable sound in Jake's mind was the desperate swish of General Sherman's sword when it came within an inch of decapitating Terminus just as Tretheway pulled him from harm's way.

Righting himself shakily, the General pointed his sword at the sky. He let loose a tormented, wild scream of rage unheard above the hellish din. The wind whipped his poorly made beard and sideburns away. His historically inappropriate cocked hat followed. A malevolent twisted glare took possession of Neil Heavenly's face. He burst through the leading edge of the flames as dramatically as any Wagnerian Valkyrie. The slow motion ended.

"Did you see who that was?" Jake shouted. In his excitement he swallowed smoke and began coughing.

"I saw." Tretheway scrambled to his feet. "Let's get out of here."

They half carried, half dragged Terminus, post and all, backwards up the sloping Incline ahead of the fire. Through sporadic holes in the flames and smoke, they were able to follow the careening railway car on its final trip.

"Gawd." Jake coughed violently. "Look at it go."

Tretheway shook his head. "I'm surprised the old tracks don't collapse."

"What's going to stop it?"

"There's a concrete wall at the bottom."

"Let's hope it holds."

"It's starting to rain," Terminus said.

They backed further up the Incline. The runaway car incredibly hugged the guiding tracks. And the tracks held. Neil Heavenly could still be seen, swaying, brandishing his sword. Twenty tons of steel coach thundered onto the city street in a fiery cloud of flying debris, with just a hint of hesitation as it made gravel out of the low concrete barrier. Heavenly disappeared. In the car's erratic journey downtown, it zigzagged from front lawn to front lawn taking out numerous bushes and small trees before finally coming to rest on a substantial traffic island three blocks away. On one zig, it almost crashed into Wan Ho's cruiser belatedly coming to the rescue.

Tretheway and Jake made it to the safe limestone shelf at the top of the Incline, still manhandling Terminus. They freed him from the post. The thin cords binding his hands and feet untied more easily than the thick hemp that had snapped the blade of Jake's knife. Jake rubbed life back into Terminus's wrists and ankles.

"Will you look at that." Tretheway viewed the panorama spread out before them.

The fire still roared fiercely despite the fitful rain. But it was running out of fuel. Already at the bottom puffs of hot ashes exploded in the air as weakened ties collapsed onto the ground below. Sirens wailed. Flashing red lights identified the emergency vehicles, several of which clustered around the smoking pyre of the Incline car. Others veered around the traffic island and raced to the Incline's base while the remainder, Wan Ho included, coursed up the mountain road on their roundabout way to the top. Stroboscopic flashes of sheet lightning eerily illuminated the whole scene.

"Too bad we're the only ones to see the Mayor's holiday extravaganza," Tretheway commented.

Jake smiled. "It looks like a long Labour Day."

The rain changed from intermittent to monsoon. They made no attempt to find shelter. Refreshingly cool rivulets made flesh-coloured streaks down their relieved, smoke-darkened faces. Tretheway looked at Jake. His wet hair stuck messily to his forehead and his white shirt, now streaked with creosote, hung halfway out of his waistband. A torn flap of pant material exposed a scratched knobby knee. One shoelace was missing.

"Do I look as bad as you?" Tretheway asked.

Jake looked down his front, then at Tretheway. "Yes," he replied.

"You okay, Miles?" Tretheway asked.

Terminus kept rubbing his wrists. He didn't answer.

"Miles," Jake repeated. "Are you all right?"

Terminus stared blankly at Jake. "I didn't mean to kill him," he said.

"You didn't," Jake said. "He rode right into the fire."

Tretheway caught Jake's eye. He shook his head. "I don't think he's talking about tonight."

Jake looked puzzled.

"It's all over now, Miles." Tretheway said.

Terminus switched his gaze to Tretheway. It was hard to tell whether he was crying in the heavy rain. Jake remembered he hadn' t put the top up on his car.

Chapter

13

Epilogue

Neil Heavenly was found on a front lawn across the street from the Incline's base. He had been catapulted from the open coach when it smashed into, and then through, the concrete barrier. His angry scowl had not relaxed in death. Except for the unusual angle of his neck, he looked remarkably unscathed. General Sherman's dress coat and 1853 cavalry sword were damaged but salvageable, much to the relief of Basil Horsborough. The cocked hat had perished in the flames.

"You mean," Addie asked, "that all these murders were really meaningless except for the last one?"

"That's right." Tretheway pushed himself forward in his soft chair and reached for a cigar.

"Only from the murderer's point of view," Wan Ho said.

Tretheway nodded. "Of course."

"Certainly not the victims," Jake said.

Tretheway nodded again. "Neil Heavenly decided to kill Miles Terminus. For reasons we'll go into shortly." He acknowledged Terminus who stood, one elbow on the mantle, sipping his tea. Five was just about capacity for the small parlour, not counting Fred.

Little information had been offered to the press. Rumours abounded. Miles Terminus had been sedated and under Doc Nooner's care for two days immediately after his ordeal, then carefully questioned by different people at different times. Tretheway's theories had proven true. A complete explanation was to appear in the *FY Expositor* starting Friday. Tonight was Thursday.

"What Neil Heavenly hoped," Tretheway continued, "was that everyone would think the burning of Terminus, or Atlanta, was just another in a series of unsolved movie murders. Inspired by *Gone with the Wind*. Which it wasn't. It was a cold-blooded, planned, revengeful act."

"Revenge for what?" Addie asked.

Tretheway held out his familiar traffic palm. "Patience. In the first movies, from *Flying Deuces* right through to *The Tower of London*, the murders were after the fact. Arbitrary choices. A big game. *Gone with the Wind* was a different story. Heavenly knew, hell everyone knew from the publicity, about Rhett Butler, Scarlett O'Hara, Ashley and especially the burning of Atlanta. Formerly Terminus. He planned backwards from *Gone with the Wind*. The only movie with a motive."

Everyone waited while Tretheway lit his cigar.

"Motive," he resumed. "Miles had better tell you about that." Tretheway looked at Terminus. "You feel up to it?"

Terminus was absently stroking the velvety folds of the dog's neck with his shoe. He stopped. "I think so." He took a deep breath.

"Neil Heavenly came to my apartment Saturday night. Late. Said he wanted to talk. He had this large duffel bag with him. He set it on the floor and pulled it open. Then started to talk about his childhood. About fond memories of his father. How he and his sister used to go for walks with his dad. How close they were. And all the time taking things out of his bag. The Union Army coat. The cocked hat. The sword and scabbard. I didn't know what to make of it."

Terminus walked across the room and gazed out the front window.

"Go on, Miles," Tretheway encouraged.

Terminus turned back to the parlour. "I asked Neil what this was all about. He said I'd find out soon enough. Then he put that damned army coat on. Never stopped talking. Now, about how his childhood had changed when his father died. Or was killed. His mood changed then. Became nasty. He told me how he and his sister had gone to an orphanage. Then foster homes. Eventually running away. And he kept dressing. Buttoning up the coat. Adjusting the cocked hat. Buckling up the sword. Then he dropped the bomb."

Terminus stared over the heads of his audience. He crossed the room once more and put his cup and saucer on the mantle.

"Would you like some more tea, Miles?" Addie asked.

Terminus shook his head.

Tretheway spoke softly. "What did he say, Miles?"

"He said he had to change his name. Asked me if I knew the Italian word for heaven. Paradiso. He said his father was Vincent Paradiso. The man that night a long time ago, when I . . . you know . . ."

"When you shot him," Tretheway finished.

"In the line of duty," Jake said.

"A policeman's lot, Miles," Wan Ho said.

"What became of the girl?" Addie tried to change the subject. "His sister?"

"She died at eighteen," Terminus said. "Pneumonia. In his arms apparently. Somehow he blamed me for that too."

"What happened then?" Tretheway persisted.

"He admitted to everything. The tricks, the pranks, the murders. Quite proud of them. From the time he stumbled across your bowler to his discovery of the Clarences' wine casks. To the point of bragging. And he told me about the finale. The burning of Atlanta. Terminus. Me. That's when I went after him. But he was expecting it. He was too quick. That damn sword." He patted the still sensitive welt on the side of his head. "Knocked me out."

"That's when he tied you up," Tretheway said. "And got you down to the truck."

Terminus nodded. "He wasn't that big, but strong. I vaguely remember the bumpy ride in the back of his truck. Under a tarp. Strong smell of gasoline. Then being hauled out. Dragged up the tracks. Every time he thought I was coming to, he whacked me with that sword. He enjoyed it too. First thing I remember half clearly is you two trying to untie me."

"Heavenly must've been hiding somewhere at the bottom when we arrived," Jake said.

Tretheway nodded. "Probably interrupted his gasoline-on-the-tracks trick."

"Must've surprised the hell out of him," Wan Ho said.

"And when we reached Miles," Jake said, "Heavenly lit the fire. Then took off."

"To the top," Tretheway said. "Where the coaches were."

"Tell me," Addie asked. "How can one small man move a heavy railway car?"

"Leverage," Tretheway answered.

"Pardon?" Addie asked.

"Take the wheel chocks away," Tretheway explained. "Then inch it along with a large crowbar."

"Easier than you think, Addie," Jake said.

"And we found a crowbar at the scene," Wan Ho said.

"Did he plan that?" Addie asked.

"I don't think so," Tretheway said. "It was out of desperation. He saw us trying to free Miles. That would ruin his whole plan. I think he went over the edge then."

"In more ways than one," Wan Ho said.

"He certainly underestimated the speed of the car," Jake said.

Tretheway and Jake looked at each other. They shared a remembered moment of Neil Heavenly's remarkable charge into the inferno.

"Well, it's all over now," Addie said. She smiled at Terminus. "I'm sure tomorrow will bring better things."

Tretheway settled back in his easy chair. He opened the *FY Expositor*. The date on the paper was the last day of the month. Tomorrow was September 1, 1939.